I0688607

NEWS AND NACHOS

A SMALL TOWN COZY MYSTERY

CARLY WINTER

Edited by
DIVAS AT WORK EDITING

Cover Design by
COVEREDBYMELINDA.COM

WESTWARD PUBLISHING / CARLY FALL, LLC

Copyright © 2020 by Carly Winter

All rights reserved.

No part of this book may be reproduced in any form or by any electronic or mechanical means, including information storage and retrieval systems, without written permission from the author, except for the use of brief quotations in a book review.

Cover by: CoveredbyMelinda.com

This book is dedicated to Christina Walker because she's awesome and sees things no one else does.
Thank you for all your help!

BLURB

Is her best friend a murderer?

When the owner of the local Mexican restaurant is found dead face down in a plate of nachos, Tilly Bordeaux, the reporter for the Tri-Town Times, is on the job.
As she dives into the life of the deceased, she uncovers seedy behavior, lies and fraud. Even though the list of those who wanted the man dead is long, the sheriff, up for reelection, is focused exclusively on Tilly's best friend, Carla, as the main suspect.
Tilly has no choice but to search for the true killer herself... before her friend is sent to prison for a crime she didn't commit.

1

———

LIFE WAS ALMOST PERFECT, until we discovered the body.

I drove to Cedarville to visit my friend Carla, which was about thirty miles west from where I lived in Oak Peak, humming a tune as the crisp, morning wind ripped through the cab of my pickup truck. My ride or die, a Golden Retriever named Tinker, sat beside me, her gaze fixed on the open road with her tongue lolling out the side of her mouth and her fur blowing in the breeze.

When we pulled up to Carla's, Tinker waited patiently for me to let her out, then bound out of the truck and ran for the house, barking as she went to announce her arrival. Mac, Carla's husband, opened the door and bent down to greet her while I meandered up the walkway.

"Hey, Tilly!" he called, flashing his big white smile while waving.

"Hi, Mac."

He gave me a quick hug and then motioned me inside.

"Carla will be ready in a minute. She's running late. As usual." Irritation laced his voice, and I smiled.

"You had to know that when you married her," I teased.

"I did, but I foolishly thought it would get better. I've been thinking about setting the clocks in the house ten minutes early and not telling her so she finally gets on schedule. She's perpetually ten minutes late."

"I don't know if that will help," I said with a laugh.

"Let me go get her and tell her you're here. Have a seat in the kitchen, or wherever you want."

I nodded and headed for the kitchen while Tinker followed. She lay under the table while I helped myself to a cup of coffee.

Footsteps sounded from the second floor as I sipped.

"I'll be down in a minute, Tilly!" Carla yelled. "I'm running late!"

"Take your time!"

After all, I had a cup of coffee to finish.

Carla's cat, Francis, strutted in and glared at Tinker from a safe distance. The white ball of fluff didn't particularly like dogs, but Tinker seemed determined to be loved. Her tail wagged, hitting my foot with a thump, thump, thump.

"Come here, Francis," I said as I patted my leg. "Tinker isn't going to hurt you."

The cat cast his stare on me, then turned around and strutted into the living room while Tinker whined.

"It's okay, girl," I said, reaching down and scratching her head. "You can't be everyone's friend, no matter how hard you try. People are going to dislike you simply because of who you are."

Definitely a hard life lesson that everyone needed to learn, even my sweet dog.

With a huff, Tinker closed her eyes and set her head on her paws, obviously disappointed that Francis had once again snubbed her attempts at friendship.

Even though winter was just around the corner and the outside air held a bit of a chill, Carla's kitchen with its grass-green paint and white cabinets reminded me of spring. I'd spent a lot of time with her at the table, and I considered her house my second home.

Ten minutes later, it sounded like a herd of elephants thundered down the stairs. But no, just Carla. How could someone so thin make so much noise?

"Sorry about that," she said. "I got caught up in my email."

"No worries," I replied as I stood and gave her a hug. "I just enjoyed a cup of coffee."

Carla leaned down and pet Tinker's head. "Are you ready to go, or should we have another?"

"Let's go," I replied, grabbing my bag. "I'll drive. You don't need your Honda covered in dog hair."

"But Tinker isn't any ordinary dog," she said in a baby voice as she continued to stroke the golden brow. "She can shed in my car at any time."

"You might change your mind on that," I said with a laugh. "I'm driving."

"Bye, Mac!" Carla yelled as we left the house.

She slid into the front seat next to me so Tinker could have the window. I loved my friend wanted my dog to be happy. Besides, we both knew Tinker would make our lives miserable if she didn't get the air blowing through her fur.

"This is really nice for you and Debbie to do," Carla said as we pulled away from the curb. "I'm sure the teachers will appreciate it."

"I hope so. They have tough jobs. They deserve to have a delicious lunch every day."

Even though I didn't have any kids and I never would unless I adopted, that didn't mean I couldn't participate in the education system. School had started a month ago, and Debbie had heard that some of the teachers were having particularly difficult classes this year. So, we decided to throw our own teacher appreciation day. I bought some burritos from the Mexican restaurant Carla managed and Debbie was baking donuts for dessert. We'd deliver all to the school this morning before the lunch bell rang.

"How's your new boyfriend?" Carla asked.

"Ugh. He's not my boyfriend. I've told you that a hundred times."

"Tilly, I don't know when you're going to admit he is."

"We're friends. That's it."

"Okay. How is he?"

"He's fine," I replied as a blush crawled up my neck and settled in my cheeks.

Derek York had moved into the house next to mine after his father had been murdered there. I found him sweet, charming, funny and so good looking, but he scared me to death. If I ever admitted we were dating, I was afraid I'd mess it all up. My marriage had crashed and burned without me even knowing and my husband had left me for a waitress he'd impregnated. If I admitted I had feelings for Derek and he ended up taking the same path as my ex-husband, I didn't know if I could handle the pain. It was easier to keep things in the friend zone, so to speak. Yes, we did hang out quite a bit and I loved being with him. But I couldn't bring myself to head into deeper waters.

"Have you kissed him yet?" Carla asked.

I glanced over at her to find a smile turning her lips, as if she enjoyed giving me the third degree. "No."

"Don't you want to?" she continued. "He's cute, Tilly. It's obvious he likes you. I don't understand why you just don't go for it."

My roadblock was my own insecurity and I didn't want a lecture from Carla on how I needed to change and trust Derek with my feelings. I already knew all these things, but I couldn't get past my inner turmoil.

"Can we just please discuss something else?" I asked.

"Fine," she replied with a sigh. "What's Debbie up to? I haven't heard from her in a couple of days."

Our friend Debbie ran the bakery, Debbie's Deliciousness, in Oak Peak, where she and I both lived. She was also the Tri-Town gossip queen. Her bakery sat two doors down from my job at the paper.

Carla lived and worked in Cedarville, a small town located about thirty miles away.

"She's good," I said. "That sugar-free line she developed is taking off like gangbusters."

"Is that one woman still working for her?"

"No. She ended up quitting."

"Debbie is a perfectionist," Carla said. "Bet she'd be really hard to work for."

"I know. Speaking of which, did you get your raise?"

"Nope."

I glanced over at Carla to find her mouth pinched in anger while she crossed her arms over her chest.

"I've been managing that restaurant for almost two years and he can't give me a raise. It's so infuriating!"

"I'm sorry, Carla. Did he give you a reason?"

"He said he couldn't afford it, but I don't understand that. Profits are up. Costs are down. We're busier than ever. I mean, most nights, I'm running the darn place."

"Is he there at all?"

"Barely. Sometimes he's there in the morning and he may work the lunchtime crowd but takes off at dinner. He may return after closing to count the money."

"Maybe you need to find a new job, Carla."

"I know. I've looked around a bit, but I haven't found anything in management. I don't want to go back to serving again."

We rode in silence for a few moments. When I pulled up in front of the restaurant, I turned to my friend. "You could always go to work for Debbie."

Carla burst out laughing. "Not on your life."

"I agree. She'd be an awful boss."

We exited the truck through the driver door and I walked around to the passenger side to give Tinker a quick snuggle. "I'll be right back."

As I followed Carla into Martinez's Mexican Fiesta, I wondered what the real reason was for the woman not getting her raise. Perhaps it all came down to Jake Martinez being a low-life scumbag. Carla had put her heart and soul into the restaurant. She'd found local farmers to purchase from, discovered ways to cut costs, and was responsible for all the scheduling. She did run the place and deserved to be compensated for it, especially if Jake showed up less and less. Thankfully, my boss, Harold, was more than happy to share the bounty the paper generated. He showed his appreciation for my hard work.

Carla pulled on the front door. When it didn't open, she fiddled with her keys while trying to find the correct one. "I'm surprised Jake or the chef, José, isn't here yet."

"Maybe they're running late as well."

She inserted the right key and unlocked the door. I went inside and allowed a minute for my eyes to adjust.

"That's weird that the lights in back are on," she said. "Jake always turns them off before he leaves. He was here last night when I went home."

Not only did the restaurant have amazing food,

but the red, yellow and green decorations were super cute. I especially liked the three-foot-high gray donkey with two six-packs of beer slung over his back in a red and yellow carrier.

"I'll be right back," Carla said.

I nodded and began my stroll through the restaurant.

Vintage black and white pictures of Mexican people lined the walls. I loved looking at them and exploring the heritage. Women making tortillas. Men with guns strapped to their sides. Kids kicking a ball around barefoot in the dirt. The flashback of history always captivated me, and as I stared at the brown, weathered faces, I wondered about their lives, their secrets, their happiness.

Without the music and the din of people talking, the restaurant felt strange... almost like its heartbeat had gone missing. A chill ran over my skin as I continued my perusal. I loved Martinez's Mexican Fiesta—they had the best food and a fantastic, upbeat atmosphere. But being in there with just Carla made me uneasy, like I was somewhere I didn't belong and I was about to get caught.

I rounded a corner and gasped. A hand dangled from a booth, but I couldn't see the rest of the person.

"Hello?" I said, afraid to approach.

No answer, and that hand didn't move.

"Carla!" I yelled, taking a couple steps back, my heart thundering.

"What?"

"Come here!"

I couldn't take my gaze from the fingertips.

She rounded the corner with my tin of burritos. "What's up, Tilly? You didn't find a bug, did you? I just had this place sprayed last week."

"No," I whispered as I lifted my arm and pointed at the hand.

"Jake?" Carla said. "Is that you?"

She hurried over to the booth and gasped, dropping the burritos. My lunch for the teachers splashed all over the floor, the red sauce covering the dangling arm. "Oh, my word!"

I raced over to her, swallowing past the fear caught in my throat. It was definitely Jake Martinez, and based on the glazed look in his eyes, the foam around his mouth, the blue tinge on his skin, he was dead. His face lay millimeters away from a plate of old nachos.

"We need to call the police," I said as I felt his neck for a pulse. Frankly, I would have been shocked to find one.

Carla stood rooted in place with her hands covering her mouth, her eyes wide with horror.

Unfortunately, this wasn't the first time I'd found a body. My neighbor, Mr. York, had been murdered during the summer and I'd discovered him with a knife sticking out of his chest. I didn't see any wounds on Jake Martinez, so perhaps he'd died of natural causes.

I pulled out my phone and dialed 9-1-1 as I studied him. The table was littered with a checkbook, receipts and ledgers, as well as a copy of the Tri-Town Times, the newspaper where I worked.

"What's your emergency?"

"We found... someone's dead. Jake Martinez in Cedarville is dead."

"Where are you at?"

"His restaurant," I replied as I the checkbook from the table to read off the address.

"We'll be there shortly."

"Let's sit outside," I said, taking Carla's hand and maneuvering her around the spilled burritos.

We plopped down on the walkway by the front door and leaned against the side of the building.

"I can't believe this," she whispered.

"Me neither," I muttered.

The second time finding a dead body upset me as much as the first. My stomach churned and I rubbed my temples with shaky hands as a headache began to form behind my eyes.

Hopefully, this time it wasn't a murder.

2

————

As two Sheriff's units pulled up, I groaned when I realized it was Sheriff Connor in one car and Deputy Byron Mills in the other. Byron and I had dated for a fleeting period and it hadn't worked out. Sheriff Connor hated me because I'd solved the murder of my neighbor, Mr. York, and he hadn't.

I would have thought he'd be happy to have a killer out of the Tri-Town community, but he'd been furious when I went to him with the murderer's recorded confession. He'd wanted me to be guilty and hadn't gotten his way.

Besides, I'd outsmarted him.

I rose to my feet and waited as they came up the walkway and Tilly barked at them.

"Why am I not surprised to find you here?" the sheriff said. "Where's the body?"

"Inside," I replied, ignoring his comment.

"What are you doing here, Tilly?" Byron asked as soon as the door closed behind the Sheriff.

"I came down with Carla to get some burritos for the teacher appreciation lunch Debbie and I were throwing at Oak Peak High School."

"And you found Jake Martinez dead?"

"Yes."

He sighed and placed his hands on his hips. With his brown hair, brown eyes, and a well-maintained physique, he was pretty to look at, but he bored me to tears. In fact, he'd given me chickens as a gift and I still didn't know whether to be offended by it or not, especially when he'd stated how, upon seeing the hens, he'd immediately thought of me.

"You're like an angel of death, Tilly," he muttered, then opened the front door.

"That's not very nice!" I yelled after him.

What a jerk. It wasn't my fault I'd found another dead person. It's not like I went out searching for them.

I glanced down at Carla, who simply stared at the cement, and I realized she may very well be in shock.

"Are you okay?" I asked.

She shook her head. "I honestly don't know. I... I can't believe this."

"Let's get you home," I said. "I'll call and make sure Mac's there."

As I pulled out my phone again, Sheriff Connor exited the restaurant.

"Since you two are here, I need your statements."

"Can it wait?" I asked. "Carla is really upset."

He glanced over at my friend then back at me. 'No, it can't wait, Tilly. You just found a dead man. We need to get your statement."

As he pulled out a notebook from his back pocket, Carla began to cry, but the Sheriff didn't seem to care, which didn't surprise me in the least.

"What are you two doing here?" he asked. "The restaurant isn't even open."

"I work here," Carla said, getting to her feet, then wiping away her tears with her fingers. "I'm the manager. Tilly had bought some burritos from us and I came here with her to fetch them."

Sheriff Connor scribbled out her statement on his notepad. "I see burritos all over the floor by Mr. Martinez."

"Yes. I dropped them when I saw him."

"So you didn't notice him when you first walked in?"

Carla shook her head. "You can't see that booth from the front door. I went to the back to get the burritos and Tilly yelled for me."

"You found the body first?" the sheriff asked, his condescending stare trained on me.

"I did. I was walking around the restaurant looking at all the old pictures. I came across Mr. Martinez and called for Carla."

"If she had waited by the front door, we would have left and never seen him," Carla said. She stared out into the street and I wondered if she wished that had happened. I know I did.

The man grunted in response. "When was the last time you saw Mr. Martinez?"

"Last night," Carla replied. "He came in just as I was leaving saying he wasn't feeling well. He thought he may have the flu."

Byron exited just when a black SUV pulled into the parking lot. All of us turned to see who it was.

A guy in his twenties eyed us as he backed into a parking spot.

"That's José," Carla said. "He's the cook."

"What's he doing here so early?" Byron asked.

"He's got to prep for the lunch crowd."

"There's not going to be any lunch crowd today," Byron said, marching over to the SUV.

José watched him approach. The next thing I knew, his tires screeched as he raced out of the parking lot.

Byron sprinted back to his car ready to take off in hot pursuit, but the sheriff called him back.

"That makes him look really guilty of something!" Byron uttered breathlessly, reluctantly approaching us.

"We can get his address and find out what he's done," the sheriff said. "No point causing havoc on the roads."

I stared at the parking place where José had been. How odd for him to take off like that. What did he have to hide? Or maybe, he just didn't trust the police?

"What else can you girls tell us?"

"That's it," I said, not bothering to correct him on the fact that Carla and I were in our thirties and certainly not girls. "We came in to get the burritos, I found Mr. Martinez, Carla walked over and dropped the burritos. I checked for a pulse, then called 9-1-1."

Connor eyed me suspiciously.

"That's it. That's what happened," I said, trying to remain pleasant. I didn't want to tangle with him.

We all turned as another car pulled in. I recognized Doctor Wheeler who lived and practiced in Cedarville and also held the title of Coroner. In his fifties, he reminded me a bit of Ironman. Super smart and good-looking, he smiled as he approached us carrying a black leather bag.

"Ladies," he said with a small nod. He then turned to the sheriff. "What do we have here?"

"Jake Martinez is dead inside. I don't see any evidence of foul play."

"Well, let me check things out."

"Can we go now?" I asked after the man walked in the building.

"Not yet," Sheriff Connor said. "Let's make sure Doctor Wheeler doesn't have any questions for you."

I sat down next to Carla again and held her hand. Her fingers felt cold and her whole body trembled worse than mine.

A moment later, an ambulance pulled up, and they unloaded a gurney, then wheeled it past us and into the building. Sheriff Connor followed them in.

"What does this mean for the restaurant?" Carla whispered. "Does it shut down?"

"I don't know."

"What do I tell the waitstaff? Why did José leave in such a hurry?"

Without an answer for her, I simply squeezed her hand.

A few minutes passed and I realized the coffee I'd drunk at Carla's had rushed right through me.

"I'm going to go inside," I said as I stood. "Nature is calling."

Carla nodded absently and pulled out her phone. "I need to call Mac and tell him what's happened."

I opened the door and stepped inside. Muffled voices became clearer as I approached the back of the restaurant where I found the doctor, sheriff, and the two EMT's with their gurney.

"I don't like the fact he's got a blue tinge to him," Doctor Wheeler said as he bent over the body. "It indicates lack of oxygen. And the foam around the mouth... that could indicate convulsions. He also seems to have died in distress. Had he been ill?"

"The girl outside said that he told her he thought he had the flu last night as she was leaving, but nachos don't seem to be something someone who was sick would eat. Could be a drug overdose as well, Doc."

"Could be," Doctor Wheeler said while stroking his salt and pepper beard. "I find it odd he thought he had the flu but came to the restaurant. He should have stayed home."

"Based on the papers, it looks like he was doing a little bookkeeping, having some nachos, then dropped dead."

I cleared my throat and everyone looked at me. "I need to use the restroom."

"Go ahead," Connor said, turning back to the doctor.

"No." Doctor Wheeler held his hand out as he stepped around the burrito mess. "I think you should wait outside."

"Why is that?" Sheriff Connor asked.

"I'm not sure this man died of natural causes."

My stomach flipped as I stared at Mr. Martinez's hand. If he didn't die of natural causes, that could only mean one other thing.

"You think someone killed him?" Connor asked.

"I'm not sure. But something here doesn't seem right to me. This man suffered a lot before he died."

"People suffer when they die of natural causes, too, Doc," the sheriff said.

"I'm very aware of that."

"You want me to treat this as a crime scene?"

Doctor Wheeler nodded and crossed his arms

over his chest as he eyed the body. "I think it would be best until I can rule out nefarious reasons."

The sheriff sighed. "All right. Byron, take Tilly outside and get the names, phone numbers, and addresses of everyone who works here from that other girl. Put some crime scene tape up across the driveway so no one can come in for lunch to get a taco."

Byron nodded then motioned for me to follow him.

"I really need to go," I said, not moving. "If you want me to stick around, then I better use the restroom."

The sheriff rolled his eyes, but then Doctor Wheeler waved me through. "Go down the next aisle, please. We don't want the scene contaminated any more than it is."

I did as instructed and pushed through the bathroom door. After doing my business, I took a moment to catch my breath as I stared at my reflection in the mirror.

The need to go home and crawl back under my covers overcame me. Maybe attempt to restart my day again in a couple of hours. Finding my neighbor, Mr. York, a few months ago had terribly upset me, and now, discovering Mr. Martinez had the same effect. Maybe the sheriff was right. I had become a dead body magnet.

At least there was the distinct possibility that Mr. Martinez had died of natural causes. With Mr. York having a knife stuck in his chest, it had been pretty obvious a murder had occurred.

I took a deep breath, washed my hands, and slipped out of the bathroom.

"Make sure you bag the nachos," Doctor Wheeler said.

"Why is that?" Connor scratched his head. "You think he choked on a chip?"

"Of course, that's a possibility." Doctor Wheeler spoke in a grave tone. "My main concern is that he's been poisoned and the substance is on the nachos."

I gasped as I hurried for the front door. Carla was still sitting back against the building with her phone in her hand.

"I'm calling everyone and telling them not to come in," she said as she stared at Byron stringing up the crime scene tape. "Did you hear anything when you were in there? What does the doctor think happened to him? Why is Byron putting up that yellow tape?"

"Oh, Carla," I said as I sat down next to her again. "I overheard them talking about a potential murder."

Carla's eyes widened and her mouth formed a perfect O. "Murder?!" she shrieked. "They think Jake was murdered? How?"

I nodded. "The doctor says maybe poisoning."

"Who would do such a thing?"

"I don't know," I replied, "but if it does come back that he was killed, you better consider a list of people you think could be responsible because the sheriff is going to want to talk to you."

"Okay," she said, her tears starting again. "I can't believe this is happening."

"You and me both, Carla. You and me both."

We sat in silence for a long while. Carla cried, and I prayed that Jake Martinez had met his maker through natural causes.

I didn't want to be involved with another murder.

3

A WEEK HAD PASSED since I'd heard from Carla and I was beginning to worry. It wasn't like her not to return my phone calls and texts. As I stood at my kitchen sink finishing up the last dishes, I glanced outside to find my neighbor, Derek York, jogging from his property to mine. A grin spread over my face and butterflies tickled my stomach. I hadn't seen much of him this week either, and it thrilled me to my toes that he had invited himself over.

"Don't you dare touch that banana bread, Belly-Belle," I said to my black cat who eyed it from the kitchen counter and actually licked her lips. "And get off there. You know better."

I tossed my dishtowel in her direction and she scampered off into the living room.

Derek smiled as I opened the front door.

"Hey, neighbor," he said, his blue eyes twinkling.

"Hi. Come in, neighbor."

"It smells wonderful in here," he said as he entered. "What are you cooking?"

"Banana bread. Do you want some?"

"I'd love a slice."

I glanced up at him as we entered the kitchen. Now his eyes looked green. I'd never understand how that happened.

"Where have you been?" he asked, taking a seat at the table. "I haven't heard from you much this week."

I grabbed two plates out of the cupboard while Tinker came bursting through the dog door and practically jumped on Derek's lap. I wasn't his only fan.

"Hey, girl!" he said, scratching behind her ears. "I've missed you, too. You need to tell your mom that we should see each other more frequently."

I filled the plates with banana bread and brought them over to the table. Derek eyed the food and licked his lips. "This looks as amazing as it smells."

"Thanks." I sat down and Tinker ran back outside. "I hope it tastes good, too."

He took a bite and grinned. "Delicious, Tilly.

You're a banana bread master. You need a crown or a sword or something."

I giggled as I took a bite myself. Not bad at all. Debbie had been encouraging me to use other sweeteners besides regular sugar, and I had to admit, I couldn't tell the difference.

"Is Tinker still in a love affair with the chickens?" Derek asked. "She tore out of here like her back end was on fire."

"Oh, yes. It's beyond ridiculous," I replied with a sigh "They just all sit there and stare at each other."

We ate in silence for a while, eating.

"So where have you been, Tilly?" he asked me again.

I shrugged and set down my fork. "Just busy. I guess you read about Carla's boss?"

"No. What happened?"

"I thought you read all my articles," I teased.

A slow smile spread across his face. "I've been busted. I must have missed the last edition. I'm sorry about that. Tell me please."

I told him about finding Jake Martinez and what Doctor Wheeler had said.

"Seriously?" His voice rose a few octaves as his mouth hung open. "Another murder? I thought the

Tri-Town area was nothing but nice folks, pretty farms, and good banana bread."

I smiled and rolled my eyes. "I'm glad you liked the bread. As for everything else, we don't know for sure. When I called to have Doctor Wheeler confirm or deny the murder, he said he had to wait for some toxicology results that he'd been able to get rushed through."

"That's too bad. I hope there isn't another killer on the loose."

"Me too. I about went crazy trying to figure out who murdered your dad."

"Which you should have left up to the police."

"They thought I did it!" I screeched. "I had to prove my innocence!"

"I know," he said, reaching across the table and giving my fingers a squeeze. "I'm very grateful for what you did. I'm just glad you weren't hurt."

Another deep blush crawled up my neck and settled in my cheeks, turning them into two balls of fire.

"Has the restaurant been closed this week?" Derek asked, withdrawing his hand from mine.

My fingers chilled, and I wished he'd grab them again. "Yes."

"I feel bad for the staff. I used to be a server. It's

tough having a job pulled out from under you like that. Especially when it happened so suddenly."

Even though Derek was a millionaire—his father left him the house and a big bank account—he didn't have an ounce of self-importance. I loved that he worried about Carla and her team.

"I'm sure it will be fine," I said. "They'll be back at work soon."

We stared at each other a quick beat, then he glanced around the kitchen. Without our voices to fill the silence, it seemed both of us felt uncomfortable.

"Do you want to watch some television?" he finally asked.

"I'd like that a lot. Do you want some hot tea? I've got chamomile or peppermint."

He grimaced as he considered his options. "Chamomile always tastes like dirt to me, but peppermint reminds me of the holidays."

"Well, it's almost Halloween. We're getting close to the holidays, so I think you should go with the peppermint."

"Sounds good. Speaking of, what are you doing for the holidays, Tilly?"

I stood and walked around the counter to prepare the tea. "I'm not sure. My parents may come out, or I'll get together with my friends. What about you?"

Remembering that he'd never spent the holidays with his father had me wanting to bite off my tongue. After Derek's mother had died, his dad had given up on him recovering from his drug habit and had wanted nothing to do with him. The situation was very sad, but I understood both sides.

"I don't know. I've been alone for the past few years or gone to a friend's house. Maybe if you're not busy we could do something together? If your parents don't come?"

"Of course," I replied as I busied myself. However, spending the holidays with Derek seemed like such a big commitment and so serious. And besides, what the heck did I buy a millionaire to put under the tree?

We were definitely friends, and he'd said he'd spent the holidays with friends in the past. Perhaps it didn't need to be something significant, but two people who enjoyed each other's company celebrating the season.

When the tea was ready, I turned to him and smiled. "What do you want to watch?"

"Let's go figure it out," he said as I handed him his cup.

I followed him into the living room and sat down on the couch. He took the cushion next to me, not too close but not too far. A comfortable distance where I didn't feel like I was being crowded, but I still had the companionship of someone I really liked.

As he scrolled through the channels, I sipped my tea. The pitter-patter of fall rain began hitting the roof and quickly turned into a downpour.

"What do you think, Tilly? A movie? Sitcom? Reality TV?"

"I don't know... let's look at—"

The pounding on my front door startled us both. The rain had blocked out the sound of the car pulling up.

Tinker barked and ran to the door as I stood and set down my cup. "That just about had me jumping out of my skin."

"Same here."

When I opened the door, dread overcame me. Byron stood on my porch. He either wanted to talk about dating me, or the murder. Neither was a topic I wanted to discuss.

"Hey, Tilly. Can I come in?"

I glanced over my shoulder toward the living room and hoped he wasn't going to start his nonsense about dating me. That would be terribly uncomfortable with Derek in the next room even though I technically wasn't dating him, either. "I-I guess so."

Thankfully, Byron wiped his wet shoes on the entry mat. The storm had quickly escalated and thunder and lightning now boomed outside.

"What's up, Byron?"

"I need to talk to you about Jake Martinez's death."

"Okay. What about it?"

"Can we sit down?"

He didn't wait for an answer, but instead grabbed a chair at the kitchen table.

I sat down across from him with a sigh. The man was beginning to irritate me. "What's going on, Byron?"

"Doc Wheeler has ruled the death a murder by poisoning."

A gasp escaped me as I brought my hand to my mouth. "Oh, my. How horrible!"

The ruling shocked me. The Tri-Town area had gone a decade without a murder, and now, even with only two dead within a few months' time, it felt like a tidal wave had hit.

"Yes. I have to go over your statement one more time for the investigation."

"Of course."

I needed to call my boss, Harold. I'd already written about Jake's death, but at that point we hadn't known for sure whether he'd been killed or had died of natural causes. This brought a whole new dimension. Everyone would want to know about the murder, which meant Harold would put out extra editions of the paper. I'd be working my tail off. The bonus I'd received from Mr. York's murder had bought me paint and new furniture, making my house my own instead of the one I'd shared with my ex-husband. I hated profiting off of other's misery, but I had a job to do.

Derek walked in and Byron turned to look over his shoulder. He quickly glanced back at me, obviously surprised by my company.

"There was another murder?" Derek asked, sitting down next to me. "Besides Jake?"

Byron cleared his throat and nodded a hello but didn't meet Derek's gaze. In fact, his cheeks turned the color of apples. Was he angry at my neighbor's presence? And if so, why? Jealousy?

Derek obviously hadn't heard the conversation correctly.

"No," I replied. "That's who we're talking about. Since I found the body, Byron wants to go over my statement again."

"Do you care if I'm here?" Derek asked, his gaze hardening as he stared at Byron. "I can go home if you like."

"Of course not," I answered quickly. When the police had thought I'd killed his father and had searched my house, Derek had offered to hire a lawyer for me. I knew he was on my side.

Byron finally met Derek's stare, and neither looked away. As the tension between them rose, I became terribly uncomfortable. The testosterone flowing within the room was enough to make me grow a mustache.

"Can we get on with it?" I asked as my heart rate increased. "The sun is getting ready to set, Byron, and you don't want to be driving back to town in this weather in the dark."

"Fine," he growled, which surprised me. He'd always been a bit of a... doormat. "Tilly, tell me what happened the day you found Jake Martinez."

I repeated my story from earlier in the week, almost word for word. "It's identical to what Carla and I told you at the restaurant."

Byron jotted down some notes on his pad then

met my gaze. "Actually, Carla's story has changed quite a bit."

A sinking feeling settled around me... as if I'd been thrown into a lake and everyone stood on shore, watching me, to see if I'd drown.

"How so?" Derek asked.

"Well, there was the fact that she had a fight with Martinez before she left on the eve of his murder and she was the last one to see him alive according to the camera recordings in the restaurant."

Both Derek and I gasped in unison.

"We're looking into it," Byron continued, "but so far, she's suspect number one."

He stood and headed for the front door as I scrambled after him. I had to know more.

"What else did she say, Byron?" I said as I opened the front door and he stepped outside.

He didn't answer, but instead glanced in the direction of the kitchen where Derek still sat, then back at me. "That guy in there is a drug addict," he hissed. "Once a drug addict, always a druggie, Tilly. Don't be stupid about who you tangle with."

"No one is tangling anywhere, Byron," I said through clenched teeth. How dare he tell me who I could and couldn't hang out with? "We're neighbors. Friends. Get over yourself."

He gave me one last glare as lightning raged over his shoulder. In that moment, with the darkening sky and the light flashing behind him, he reminded me of a serial killer and I slammed the door.

Not that I'd ever seen a serial killer in real life that I knew about, but he definitely reminded me of the ones in the movies.

Derek came up behind me and laid his hands on my shoulders. "Are you okay?"

I nodded but the dread wouldn't leave me. Carla hadn't called for a reason, and now I realized what it was.

The police were questioning her about the murder. I knew exactly how helpless and desperate that felt.

Did I think Carla did it?

No.

But the fact that she may have been the last one to see Jake Martinez alive and she'd argued with him didn't bode well for her.

I laid my hand over one of his and gave it a squeeze. "Do you think they're trying to pin this on her?"

Derek sighed and slowly spun me around. "Beats me. But we'll help out any way we can, okay? In any way that won't put us in danger."

I stared into his green eyes and wanted to collapse at his feet with the sympathy and caring I saw there. Instead, I wrapped my arms around his waist and buried my face in his chest. Did that mean him hiring a lawyer? Us taking care of Carla and Mac's cat? I didn't know.

However, I did appreciate the strong arms around me and the calm feeling they gave me.

It was our first hug, which terrified me, yet felt wonderfully comforting.

With a sigh, I stepped away. Carla needed my help.

I wouldn't let her go down for a murder she didn't commit.

4

THE NEXT DAY, I went into work early to plan Carla's defense. Oak Peak Avenue remained quiet in the early fall morning, and I scrunched up my nose at all the Re-elect Sheriff Connor signs that had been put up overnight. He wouldn't get my vote if he were the last man standing.

I didn't know much about Jake's death, but the fact that Byron had said Carla's story had changed and she'd been the last one to see Martinez alive didn't sit well with me at all. I had to find out what Carla had told the police, figure out a plan of action, then help her in any way I could. That Sheriff wouldn't want to go into the last weeks of his reelection campaign with an unsolved murder. Instead, he'd want to run on his pristine record of fighting for justice and keeping the Tri-Town area free of crime.

Or something stupid like that.

After filling my coffee cup, I sat at my desk and redialed Carla for the third time that morning. When she picked up, she didn't bother to try to hide her annoyance with me.

"What is wrong with you, Tilly? Has someone died or something?"

"I've been trying to get a hold of you for a week and you haven't returned any of my calls."

"I'm sorry," she said with a sigh. "I've been so busy. The police gave Jake's daughter permission to open up the restaurant, but we don't have enough staff. Some went and found other jobs. I'm scrambling."

"Jake has a daughter?"

"Yes. Her name's Sophia. She just turned eighteen. The restaurant is hers now."

My heart ached for the girl. I recalled my own father's death when I was ten, and it had been a horrible, difficult time. Even at eighteen, the loss would be insurmountable.

I'd never met the girl, but I wanted to help her, as well as Carla.

"What positions do you need to fill?" I asked.

"Mac is going to do the dishes tonight. I hired a guy for that job, but he can't start right away. Thank goodness José is here to cook, or we wouldn't be able to open. Jake's brother, Tony, is here to help José in the kitchen, I guess I need one more server and someone to hostess."

"Hmm... let me call you right back. I have an idea."

I quickly dialed Derek, who unlike Carla, picked up on the first ring.

"This is a nice surprise," he said. "What's up?"

"You said last night you'd worked as a restaurant server."

"Yes, for many years."

"Do you think you can do it again? For Carla? She's trying to reopen the restaurant but needs some help."

"Sure. I can do that. Just let me know when to be there."

I loved how he didn't hesitate for a second to help my friend.

"Thanks, Derek. I really appreciate it. I'll call you back and let you know what time."

I immediately returned the phone call to Carla.

"Derek has serving experience and I can take over the hostess job," I said without preamble. It was evident that Carla was under a lot of stress and didn't have time for chit-chat. "What time should we be there?"

"Oh, wow," she said with a sigh. "Thank you. This will help so much. Can you guys be here at four? We're opening for dinner at five."

"Yes, Ma'am. We'll see you then."

At some point in the evening, I would corner Carla and find out what she told the police. But for the time being, I had to concentrate on work.

Harold walked in and I revealed Jake's death being declared a murder.

"Here we go again, huh?" he said, rubbing his hands together. "We've got to move our output into high gear."

"Yep," I said with a sigh. "Here we go again."

I'D NEVER DONE a day of hostessing in my life, but I had been a server for a short time when I lived in Louisiana. I'd always thought the hostesses had the easy job and I could do it in my sleep. When Derek and I arrived, Carla introduced us to José, the chef, and Jake's brother, Tony. Neither seemed overly friendly, but both expressed their thanks for us helping out.

After Carla introduced us to Jake's daughter, Sophia, who would be waiting tables with Derek, we were ready to go. She seemed sweet and was one of the prettiest girls I'd ever seen with her long black hair and wide brown eyes.

"I'm really sorry for your loss," I said.

"Thanks. It's been a tough week, but we've got to keep moving forward, no matter how hard it is."

Sweet, pretty, and I was a little surprised by her maturity. I could see the pain in her eyes, but they remained dry. No tears for her.

As Carla opened the front door, my hands shook with nerves. I hoped I wouldn't mess up, but really... how hard could it be?

A line of customers filed in and I smiled and greeted them. After grabbing a few menus, I sat the first group of people, and went back for the second. Carla jumped in and helped me, and everyone was seated within minutes. Almost every table was full.

"What about that booth where we found Jake?" I whispered. "We can sit someone there if anyone else comes in."

Carla shook her head. "No. Not tonight. We never sat anyone there before. It's kind of out of the way and he always used it for himself. Let's leave it empty."

The restaurant was packed, and I wondered if people knew that someone had been killed there, or if that was the reason they'd come. We'd published an article about Jake's death earlier in the week, but nothing had come out then about it being a murder. I assumed the small-town gossip vine in Cedarville was as active as the one in Oak Peak, so people could definitely be aware of the tragedy. I didn't hear much about it as I hustled during the evening, which surprised me. Should I be impressed that very few talked about the untimely death or horrified that they remained silent about it? If it were me or anyone I knew, we'd be talking about it non-stop and trying to figure out where in the restaurant Jake had died.

I pitched in where I could—busing tables, wiping them down, passing drink orders to the servers—which also gave me the opportunity to watch Derek in action. He smiled and joked with the patrons and everyone seemed to like him. He was quick, efficient, and friendly. My heart melted with appreciation for him helping out.

Overall, I didn't make too many mistakes. I miscounted how many tables were available a couple of times and had to lead people back to the front door instead of seating them. I did drop some plates in the kitchen, but with Mac's help, I quickly cleaned them up, and thankfully, no one had been hurt.

The night remained steady. Everyone seemed to need their Mexican food fix and I even saw some people from Oak Peak. Although we were supposed to close at nine, Carla gave us the go ahead to keep seating people. At 9:30, I had to turn people away and ask them to come back the next evening. I couldn't help but wonder what it would do to the customer influx when they found out Jake had been poisoned. Would they stay away, or keep coming?

As I was busing a table, I heard men yelling in the kitchen. I glanced over to find Derek also staring that way, and Carla ran through the restaurant to see what had happened.

I followed to find Mac trying to calm another man who I'd never seen. Wearing jeans, a plaid shirt, and a denim jacket, I pegged him to be about fifty years old. The stench of booze emanating from him was so strong, it smelled like he had more whiskey than blood coursing through his veins.

"Lower your voice, Jerry!" Mac said through gritted teeth. "We've got customers out front!"

"Where is it?" he yelled. "Where's my check?"

"Jerry!" Carla hissed. "Please! Stop this now!"

"No! Jake owes me money! He said he'd have it to me a week ago, and then he died! I need to get paid!"

"I know," Carla said as she laid her hand on his arm, obviously trying to soothe the man. "We're doing the best we can. It's our first night open since Jake's death. Let me settle up after the customers leave and I'll see what I can do, okay?"

Jerry shook his head as he pursed his lips. "I thought things would be different after Jake died. You seem like an honest woman, Carla. I expected more from you, but I can see you're no different from that slimeball."

"Get out before we call the police," Mac growled, stepping between Carla and Jerry. "You don't talk to my wife that way."

Jerry mumbled something under his breath, then turned and stalked out the back door. Carla glanced around as tears welled in her eyes. "Let's finish up the service. Please, everyone, go back to work."

Her stare landed on Sophia. "We need to pay him," Carla said. "It's not right."

"He can wait," Sophia said, then walked out into the dining room.

José and Tony went back to cooking and Mac returned to the sink. Carla and I were left staring at each other.

"Who was that?" I asked.

"It's one of the vendors. He's a local farmer. I made a deal with him and got some of the meat we use at a discounted price. Jake owes... I should say, owed him money."

"A lot?"

"A good amount," she said with a shrug.

"Why doesn't Sophia want to pay him?"

"She says she needs a paycheck and so does everyone else who works here."

I nodded, understanding that Sophia wanted to pay the employees first. But I imagined the farmers would be talking and word would get out that Jake hadn't paid, and neither had his daughter. That wouldn't bode well for supplies.

"You know you don't have to give me anything," I said. "I'm here because I want to help you out."

Carla's shoulders sagged in relief. "Thanks so much, Tilly. I really appreciate that."

I'd ask Derek if he'd be willing to work tonight without a paycheck. I had a feeling he'd say yes—he certainly didn't need the money—but I didn't feel comfortable telling Carla that he would do so before I made sure.

I returned to the dining room and glanced around. The crowd had finally thinned out and we only had a couple of tables left. I helped bus the dishes and scrub the tabletops. My feet hurt, and I couldn't wait to get home and snuggle with Tinker and Belle.

For a brief moment, I imagined throwing Derek in that mix, like we were a couple. My stomach twisted, my cheeks warmed, and I became so nervous, I dropped a handful of silverware.

"What was the deal with that guy?" Derek asked as he bent over and picked up my mess. Then he grabbed some cups from the table and placed them in the busing tub.

"Thanks for helping me out," I said. "Jake owed him money. Well, the restaurant owes him money."

"The guy looked like he'd been hitting the bottle hard."

"Yeah, I thought I smelled alcohol."

"He's a local guy?"

"Yes. A farmer they used for their meat supply."

Derek nodded then glanced around the restaurant. "Did you hear what he said?"

I replayed what I remembered about the conversation, then shook my head. "About what?"

"About Jake's death. He said that he thought things would be better once Jake was dead."

I gasped and set down the rag I'd been using to clean the table. "Oh, my gosh. You're right!"

"But what does it mean? Does it mean he killed Jake and thought he'd get his money from Carla and Sophia, or that he heard about the death and only then figured he'd receive his payment?"

"I... I don't know."

"Me neither, but it's something we should let the police know."

"Yes. Thanks for pointing that out."

"Just please promise me you're not going to get involved, Tilly. You don't need to be solving this murder. Let the police do it."

"Don't worry, I will. I have no intention of confronting another killer."

He smiled, winked, then walked away.

I wished the thought of the two of us being a couple didn't make me so nervous. Derek cared for me, and it both terrified me and warmed my soul. I had thought Tommy cared as well, but I'd been wrong. Or maybe he'd had for a little while, then lost interest. I just wished my insecurities didn't hold me back in considering a relationship with Derek. It was so much easier just being neighborly friends. In the end, I wanted to move beyond the current situation with him, but I panicked at the thought of being hurt again.

I sighed as Carla walked over and laid her hand on my shoulder. 'We're about ready to close," she said. "Everything okay?"

"It's fine, Carla. Except, when we shut this place down, you and I are going to take a seat and you're going to share with me exactly what you told the police."

She furrowed her brow and shook her head. "No. I'm going home. I'm exhausted."

"I'm tired too, but Byron told me you're suspect number one. We need to talk, Carla, or you may go down for Jake's murder."

5

"ARE you sure you don't want me to wait for you?" Derek asked with a yawn. "It's not a big deal." I'd told him I needed to talk to Carla in private, so I'd spend the night at her house. "I really don't mind."

"Seriously? You'd do that for me?"

"Yep. I'll just take a snooze in the parking lot. I'm either getting old or I didn't remember how hard serving is."

I smiled as he squeezed my hand. "Thanks. We shouldn't be very long."

After Derek left the building, I turned and found Carla sitting in a booth with a stack of papers while the kitchen staff finished up in back.

"What's all that?" I asked as I slid on the seat across from her.

"Bills that I don't know how I'm going to pay."

"Why is it your responsibility? Sophia is the owner now, right? Shouldn't she be in charge of that?"

"She's barely eighteen," Carla said with a sigh. "She's begging me to help her navigate all this."

I folded my hands on top of the table, the din of José and Tony chatting in the kitchen wafting through the now empty restaurant. Carla had far more important things to worry about than someone else's bills. "What did you tell the police? Byron said your story changed."

"Not by much. I told the truth. That Jake and I had argued and he was here when I left."

"What was the argument about?"

"My pay. I told him I felt like he was taking advantage of me."

That's because he was, but I didn't voice my opinion.

"Byron told me the sheriff likes you for the murder."

Carla rolled her eyes. "That's just stupid, Tilly. Byron's probably just trying to get under your skin because you're spending so much time with Derek."

I pursed my lips together and shook my head.

"That may be, but you need to think about others who would want to hurt Jake."

"Why? I'm innocent. The truth will prevail. I'm not going to jail for something I didn't do."

"It happens all the time, Carla," I said, getting angry. "There are plenty of innocent people in prison."

"Well, I'm not going to sit here and make up stories about others so I don't go to prison."

"I'm not asking you to lie or to finger anyone. I'm asking you to consider other options of who may have killed Jake. That's it."

"Don't get snippy with me, Tilly. I don't have the energy to deal with it tonight."

"Right now I'd like to knock you over the head with a two-by-four of common sense. You're being downright stupid. Have you forgotten that Sherriff Connor tried to pin Mr. York's murder on me? And now there's talk of him doing the same to you? You have to be prepared, Carla, with other names for him."

She opened her mouth to argue, but then sighed and shut her eyes, placing her head in her palms. I waited patiently, hoping the disagreement had resolved and she saw things my way.

"He's up for reelection in just a few weeks, Carla.

He's going to want this murder solved. He won't want to go into the election with this hanging over him."

"That's something you'd see on television," she said as she laid her hands on top of the papers. "That's not real life."

"Let's pretend it's real life, okay? Just humor me."

She stared at me a beat.

"Come on, Carla."

"I don't like speaking ill of the dead."

"No one does, may Jake Martinez rest in eternal peace. But you could be saving your own hide here."

"Fine," she replied with a sigh. "Jake was not a very nice person to a lot of people. Conflict seemed to follow him around."

"Like what? Who?"

"Just thinking about the people who work here... he fought all the time with Sophia."

"About what?"

"Everything," she said with a sigh. "Especially the fact that she was dating José."

I furrowed my brow. "José the chef?"

"Yes."

"He looks like he's close to thirty years old! Didn't you tell me she's eighteen?"

"He's twenty-seven, and they started dating right when she turned eighteen."

I knew my jaw hung open. "That's quite the age gap."

"Yes. And Jake threatened to call the police on José and have him arrested, even though she's eighteen. Jake was thinking about trying to get José put away for statutory rape, but he couldn't. Both Sophia and José swore they weren't having sex. They were hanging out, and that's it."

"Do you believe that?"

"No. Not at all. It's complete nonsense. Anyone can see that they're lovers."

"Wow. I get why Jake would be upset about that."

"I do, too," Carla replied. "Jake wanted to protect his little girl, even though she was legally an adult. It was a huge fight between the three of them, and José said he loved Sophia and nothing would keep them apart."

"What did Sophia say?"

"That if her father tried to separate them, they'd run away and he'd never see her again."

"Why did Jake keep José employed here?"

"Because he's an amazing chef and good for business. That and Sophia begged and pleaded for Jake to keep him."

"Well, that's dramatic, but it doesn't mean that José murdered him."

"It's possible. I overheard him tell Sophia that if her father tried to keep them apart, he'd kill Jake."

I gasped and brought my hand to my mouth. "What did Sophia say?"

Carla shrugged and yawned. "I don't know, Tilly. I didn't hear her answer. Can we go home now?"

"Just a couple more questions," I replied. "What about the farmer that was here? What was his name?"

"Jerry."

"Derek pointed out something he said that made me wonder about him."

"What's that?"

"He said he thought things would be better after Jake's death. Derek was wondering if that meant he'd killed Jake and hoped you'd pay him, or if he'd heard about Jake's death and then hoped you'd pay him."

Carla ran her hand over her black curls and released a ragged breath. "I don't know what he meant. Jake fought with Jerry all the time. When I first started using him and Jake was late paying him, Jerry said he'd never supply the restaurant again. Then Jake paid in full, and Jerry delivered us more meat. It was a never-ending battle between the two."

"Maybe Jerry got tired of it."

"Perhaps. I would have."

We sat in silence for a moment as I contemplated our new suspects. Both would have to be looked at more in-depth, and I wished I had my notepad so I could jot down all the information.

"Anyone else you can think of?" I asked.

"Well... I haven't known Jake's brother, Tony, for very long. Word is that he works at a farm down south. He's really quiet and got out of prison about a year ago."

"Prison? For what?"

"I don't know," Carla said with another yawn. "I don't ask, and no one tells me. It's none of my business. I barely know the guy, but he's always been nice to me."

"Okay... I'll find out what he did."

"Why? He's fine, Tilly. Look, I just really want to go home."

"Okay," I said, standing. "Let me know if you think of anything or anyone else."

She muttered something under her breath as I strode toward the front door. Why couldn't she see I wasn't trying to pester her or stick my nose where it didn't belong, but I was attempting to help her?

The fall night air smacked me in the face like a cold washcloth. Winter was definitely around the corner.

I smiled as I slid into Derek's warm SUV, then placed my hands in front of the heating vents.

"Everything go okay?" he asked.

"Yes. I don't understand why Carla stays there. The place seems to be crazy with drama."

Derek pulled out of the parking lot and on to the main road. In a few miles, we'd hit the two-lane highway that would take us back to Oak Peak.

"Did you ask her why?"

"No. But I should."

"What did she say? Could she think of anyone else who wanted Jake dead?"

"Yes. José and possibly even Jake's own daughter."

Derek listened intently as I recapped my conversation with Carla about José and Sophia.

"Jake didn't have a leg to stand on legally, but I get why he'd be upset. That's a big age gap."

"It is," I replied. "It looks like José is preying on Sophia, but who knows? Jake just wanted to protect his daughter."

"José seemed like an okay guy, so I'm surprised

that he'd say he'd kill Jake if he tried to keep him and Sophia apart."

I hadn't really talked to José, but I kept thinking about his actions when Carla and I had found Jake's body. He'd pulled into the parking lot and then sped off when he saw the cops. Byron had said it made him seem guilty, and I had to agree. At the time I wasn't sure what he was guilty of, but now, I was considering him for the killer.

Maybe Jake had threatened to fire José if he didn't stop dating Sophia and José had followed through on his warning.

"What's going through that pretty head of yours?" Derek asked.

I smiled and glanced over at him. "I was just thinking that José had a really good reason to murder Jake."

"You know, I was thinking the same thing. Not only has he cleared the way to be with Sophia, but he's kept his job and once she gets her footing in running the business, he'll practically be a co-owner."

Dang, Derek had a smart head on his shoulders.

"That didn't occur to me, but you're right. He wins all the way around. He gets the girl and the restaurant."

"We should tell Byron about it," Derek said. "Just to let him know there are definitely other avenues to explore when searching for the murderer."

"I'm sure José is on Byron's radar already."

When I told Derek about José leaving the parking lot, he nodded enthusiastically. "If that doesn't scream guilt, I don't know what does."

As he pulled into my driveway, I didn't want our time together to end, but when I glanced at the clock, I saw it was past midnight. I had to get to bed in order to be somewhat coherent in the morning for work.

"Thanks for helping out tonight," I said. "I really appreciate it, and I know Carla did, too."

"Sure. Let me know if she needs my amazing serving skills again."

I nodded, remembering that I needed to ask him about forgoing a paycheck. It made me uncomfortable to do so, but I had to let Carla know one way or the other.

"There's something I need to ask you," I said, tucking a stray piece of hair behind my ear.

"What's that?"

"Well, it seems like the restaurant is in bad financial shape. I told Carla that I didn't need to be paid for tonight, and I was wondering if you'd do the same."

He stared at me a moment with a small grin, his eyes shining in the dashboard light.

"You're really sweet, Tilly," he said, his voice quiet. "No, I don't need the money."

"Thank you."

He sighed and stared out the front window.

"What's wrong?" I asked, now worried I'd somehow offended him. "If you want to get paid, that's fine."

"No, it's not that. I was hoping you were going to ask me something else."

"Like what?"

He turned to me again, his face serious. "I was hoping you were going to ask if it would be okay for you to steal a kiss from me."

My heart fluttered and I became incredibly warm and dizzy. Then I realized I wasn't breathing. Air escaped my lungs in a loud whoosh.

I had no idea what to say, so I opened the door and escaped.

Tears stung my eyes as I rushed into my home and Derek drove away. I wanted to kiss him. I wanted to feel confident enough to do so, but fear held me back.

After shutting the door behind me, I pet Tinker while the tears fell. I hated my ex for making me so insecure. I had a perfectly good man who wanted to date me, and I couldn't get past being left for a pregnant waitress.

And the fact that I'd just bolted from the car like he'd asked me to cut off my own arm... I wouldn't be the least bit surprised if he never wanted to see me again.

Besides, I didn't have time for romance—at least that's what I kept telling myself. Another murder in the Tri-Town area should hold all my attention. I had to report on it and also hope the sheriff actually did his job instead of pinning the murder on my best friend.

6

I SPENT most of the night staring at the ceiling, listening to Tinker's soft snores and berating myself for acting like such an idiot. I liked Derek. A lot. Fear held me back, and I had to push past it.

After a fitful sleep, I rose before my alarm sounded and glanced out the window. Derek's house remained dark in the early morning hours before the sun rose. He had nowhere to be since he didn't have a job, but instead, possessed a stack of money in the bank. I shivered in the cool air and realized I'd need to turn on the heat before long. I wished I could stay in bed as well, but no, as the only reporter in the Tri-Town area, I was needed, especially with a murder investigation going on. All I required was a cape, and everyone could call me Superman.

After a long, hot shower, two cups of coffee and some toast, I felt more awake, yet the pit of despair I'd developed after my horrible treatment of Derek continued to grow. The wind howled outside, and I held Belle as we stood at the window watching the autumn leaves tousle in the wind. Tinker stood on her hind legs with her paws on the windowsill next to me. She whined, and I knew she had to go to the bathroom but didn't want to go outside. My golden retriever was a summer girl and hated anything but bright, sunny days.

"Please don't go in the house," I said, sipping my third cup of coffee. "The wind isn't going to hurt you. You can be brave."

I glanced down at her and her up at me. Belle meowed in my arms. "Are you two judging me? If you are, you're right. I should follow my own advice and be brave with Derek. I know that. But this is one of those do as I say, not as I do, situations." I set Belle down and she and Tinker curled up on the couch together. "Please do your business outside, Tinker. Okay?"

She stared at me a moment, then shut her eyes. I'd been dismissed. "You two have a great day. Love you both."

After setting my coffee cup in the sink, I walked

out the front door. The wind made it difficult to shut, and I had to really yank on it. I screamed as I slammed my finger and tears welled in my eyes. After getting the door locked, I stared at the tip of my finger. Broken? Just bruised? I wiggled it and it seemed to be moving okay without too much pain, so hopefully just a bad bruise.

As I drove past Derek's house, I vowed that I would visit him after work and apologize for my quick exit the previous night. I would tell him my fears and let him know I wanted to date him, but I really needed to take it slow. My anxiety and fragile ego couldn't take some big whirlwind romance that crashed and burned in tragedy.

As I pulled up in front of the office, I noted Harold was already in. That meant he would be full of high-fuel octane and going a million miles per hour.

I, however, needed another cup of coffee. And frankly, as I eyed Debbie's Deliciousness, I was craving a donut. Yet, in my current state, I didn't feel strong enough to resist. Even though I wanted to try to eat away my negative emotions, I wouldn't.

Debbie carried a wonderful line of sugar free products made with wholesome sweeteners, but I didn't possess the strength to decline the real thing.

I'd skip a visit to the bakery for the time being. Maybe later this afternoon I'd be strong enough to say no. My weight loss wouldn't be derailed, even by a murder and my own fear of dating a man I really wanted to get to know better.

When I entered the office, I felt the electricity in the air before I laid eyes on Harold.

"Tilly! Good morning!"

"Morning."

"We've got a lot of work to do, my fair lady reporter."

"Yes, we do."

I knew that translated to I had articles to write and he had ad space to book, checks to cash, and layouts to complete. I'd be lying if I didn't admit his enthusiasm caught on and my heart beat a little faster. We'd been through the preliminaries of the investigation yesterday, but I knew Harold wanted to sink his teeth into the nitty-gritty of it all.

"Where do you want me to start?" I asked as I sat down at my desk.

"Let's get our plan together."

I nodded as he pulled over a chair.

"We know for sure Jake's death is a murder," he said, his pen poised over a piece of paper.

"Yes."

"You had said that Byron mentioned a poisoning. Do we know that for certain? And if so, what is it?"

"We know it's poisoning, but we don't know what kind."

"And they're still looking at Carla Marker for a suspect."

I gripped my pen so hard, I thought it may break. "She didn't do it, and I'm not writing anything that mentions her name."

Harold sat back in his chair and arched his brows. "Why not?"

"She's my friend. I know she didn't do this."

"I see," Harold said, tapping one end of his pencil, then the other. "You can't base your reporting off your emotions. We work with facts, and right now, she's suspect number one, according to the sheriff."

"Understood. But she didn't do it. I'm not going to ruin her life over what Sheriff Connor may think. I'm happy to write about facts, and the facts are that Carla is innocent."

Harold rose from his chair and paced the small space of our office, his arms crossed over his chest.

"Well, I think we need to go with—"

Both of us turned as the door opened, and I rolled my eyes when the sheriff came into view.

"Harold! How's everything going?" he asked as he strode over to my boss and shook his hand.

"Good, thank you. You remember Tilly, don't you?"

Harold pointed over the sheriff's shoulder at me.

The man hadn't seen me tucked away around the corner from the door. As he faced me, his smiled faded.

"Of course," he said, tipping his hat to me. "How could I forget Tilly?"

I forced my lips into a grin and waved.

"What brings you around, Sherriff Connor?" Harold asked.

"Well, I wanted to check on this fantastic publication and see how things were going."

"We're fine. Just fine," Harold answered.

"Excellent," Connor said. "And how's the wife?"

"Nadine is super. Thank you for asking."

I glanced out the window and noted all his reelection posters that had been hung all around town onto light poles and in the store windows of his supporters. His trip to our office wasn't a friendly check-in. He never came to visit. He wanted an endorsement and knew that the paper would be in great demand while we kept the public informed on the murder.

An uncomfortable silence fell over the room as Harold and I waited for the man to reveal his true reason for coming over.

He cleared his throat. "As you know, I'm running for reelection. My opponent is a man from Little River. Big city cop from Chicago who moved here a couple of years ago. The man hasn't lived in the area long enough to understand our community."

Harold nodded and pursed his lips for a moment. "Well, I've decided we're going to run a piece on both of you to help the folks in the Tri-Town area make informed decisions. Help everyone get to know him and his policies, his background and accomplishments, as well as get a refresher about our esteemed sheriff."

I could practically see the proverbial smoke shooting from Connor's ears. "Well, I think I've done a mighty fine job as sheriff, and I was hoping your paper would endorse me. The townspeople know me and it would make a difference if our local paper gave me the thumbs up. Put the final nail in the guy's coffin, so to speak."

"Well, it's our policy that we don't endorse any candidate," Harold said with a smile. "We like to remain impartial. But as long as you're here, why don't we get that interview done that I was just discussing?"

Sheriff Connor fisted his hands at his sides while trying to hide his anger. "Of course, sure," he said. "Let's get right to it."

I pulled out my notepad as Harold rolled over a chair for him. The sheriff sat in the middle of our small office while my boss took a seat behind his desk, and I remained at mine.

"Let's start with a little background on you," Harold said, his pen poised above his paper.

As Sheriff Connor droned on about how he'd grown up in the Tri-Town area and how much he loved it and wanted to dedicate his life to the people, relief swept through me that I didn't have to do the interview alone. Last time I'd sat down to talk to the sheriff, he'd accused me of murder, called me names, made me feel incompetent and foolish, and told me I was stupid.

But now the blowhard was in my territory, and I had some questions.

"We have another murder in the Tri-Town area," I began. "The second one in six months after going a decade without one. Why do you think that is?"

"I don't know. Maybe we've had some unsavory characters move in over the past couple of years."

With me relocating with my ex-husband just over three years ago, I had a feeling that jab may be directed at me, but I decided to ignore it.

"How's the investigation going?" I asked. "Are you any closer to finding a suspect?"

"Oh, yes. We've got one in particular who looks interesting."

"And do you know what kind of poison was used to kill Mr. Martinez?"

"We're waiting for final testing to come in, but we'll nab her. We've almost got all the evidence we need to arrest her. I've got my best men on the case."

I bit my lip and tried to remain professional, and it wasn't easy. "Is the 'she' you're referring to Carla Marker?"

Sheriff Connor smiled at me, but then said, "No comment."

In my book, I had hit the nail on the head.

"You know she didn't do it and you're barking up the wrong tree, don't you?" I asked.

"Actually, no. I think we are definitely at the right tree."

"Based on what?" I asked. "Based on the fact she had a fight with Jake?"

"We actually have a lot of evidence against her," Connor said, his face turning red.

"Like what?"

"It's none of your damned business, Matilda!" he shouted as he shot to his feet. "You keep your nose out of this murder investigation. Do you understand me?"

I stared at him for a beat and shook my head. "Have you even bothered to question Jake's daughter? Or her boyfriend? Do you even know who she's dating? Do you know that there's been trouble between the three of them?"

A flicker of doubt crossed his face, and I had my answer. He was zoned in on Carla and he wasn't willing to look anywhere else. The so-called evidence he had on her was enough for him.

"Are we done here, Harold?" the sheriff grumbled.

"Yes, sir. I believe we are."

When the door shut, Harold glanced over at me and shook his head. "You have to let the case play out, Tilly. You can't nose around in police business."

"I know that," I said, getting to my feet.

But that was exactly what I intended to do.

7

THE SHERIFF'S visit had only dampened my mood further. I marched over to Debbie's ready to dive headfirst into a plate of donuts and eat away my anger, which the man had caused, and also the fury brewing from my actions with Derek the previous evening.

I walked in and Debbie waved, but her smiled quickly faded and she shook her head. She could see my mood had gone south. After pointing to a table, she went back to helping the customers. When everyone had been taken care of, she came over with two coffee cups.

"Did you want anything else?" she asked.

"One of your crème donuts would be great."

She ran her hand through her spiky red hair

before meeting my gaze. "As your friend, I'm going to remind you that you asked me to keep you away from sugar, but if you want one, I'll go get it."

I sighed as I stirred cream in my cup. I'd lost so much weight just by cutting out all the sugar, and I shouldn't start eating it now. No more emotional eating. I only wished I could be like Debbie, who owned the bakery and ate whatever she wanted and still remained rail-thin.

"You're right. I don't want it."

"Can I offer you a sugar free pastry?" Debbie asked. "I just took some chocolate donuts out of the oven."

"No. Not now. But thanks."

"Okay then. What's got you madder than a wet cat?"

I leaned over the table and whispered, "We've got to figure out who killed Jake Martinez, Debbie."

"Why? Isn't that what the police are for?"

"Sheriff Connor was just in our office. He's not looking anywhere but at Carla. I was right. He wants to clear the murder before the election comes up."

"Did he actually say that?" Debbie asked as her eyes widened. "Seriously?"

"Not those exact words, but he said they were

waiting for final testing to come back and they had all the evidence they needed to put her away."

"Did you ask if he was talking about Carla?"

"Yep."

"And?"

"And he gave me that smug smile that makes me want to punch him in his condescending face and said, no comment."

Debbie took a long sip of her coffee, then set her cup down. I swear she ran on caffeine and sugar. "That doesn't mean anything, Tilly."

"You'd agree with me if you saw him answer," I said, rolling my eyes. "Believe me, I know. He's going after Carla."

"Okay, so let's pretend you're right. What should we do?"

"I need you to do what you do best: ask questions, gossip and gather information. Everyone talks to you. Listen to what people are saying."

Debbie nodded and glanced around the store once more, checking on her customers. "I do that all day long."

"I know. Just listen for anything that may connect anyone but Carla to the murder."

"Looks like the sheriff is coming in here," she murmured as she rose from the table. "Don't move,

Tilly. The last thing we need is a confrontation between the two of you. I'll be right back. He never stays to chat."

I turned to see the man out on the sidewalk talking to someone, then enter the store. He said hello to a few of the patrons while he shook hands. If there had been any babies, he'd have kissed their foreheads. He glanced over at me but didn't approach. I'd been raised to respect authority, but the man had tried to pin a murder on me, and now he had my friend in his sights. My grin widened as his smile faded. I imagined he thought of me as the bee that wouldn't go away, always buzzing around in his peripheral vision.

I had every intention of stinging him.

After Debbie made small talk and gave him his coffee, he left and she returned to the table.

"He's out trying to get re-elected, not solve a murder," she said.

"I told you. He says he's got his best men on the case."

Debbie snorted and rolled her eyes. "Does he mean Byron? If so, we're all in a heap of trouble. Byron couldn't find someone's finger if it was poking him in the eye."

A giggle escaped me, and my heavy mood lightened just a bit. It felt good to laugh. I could always count on Debbie.

I glanced at my watch. The morning had quickly turned into the afternoon and I really had to get my butt in gear. Harold would be gnashing his teeth looking for articles on the murder.

"I need to get back to the office," I said with a sigh.

"Don't worry about getting information," Debbie said as she patted my hand. "I'll keep my ears open and report back whenever I hear something interesting. We'll get Carla out of this mess, I can promise you that. We've caught one killer, and there's no reason why we can't catch a second."

When I walked outside, the sheriff was standing on the sidewalk across the street shaking hands with people coming out of the hardware store. He didn't care who committed the murder as long as he remained sheriff, and that didn't bode well for Carla.

I FINISHED my day with a master plan in place of interviews that I needed to get. First up would be Sophia, Jake's daughter. With a little help from Google, I found her address within seconds and decided the best way to approach her was without an appointment. I didn't want her to know I would be coming.

As I drove home, my palms began to sweat and my heart thundered. I really didn't want to talk to Derek, but I felt so awful for scampering away like a deer caught in the headlights. I had to explain myself.

While passing his house, I saw him out back talking to Minnie. Apparently, her stupid cows, Tulip and Sunflower, had gotten loose again and meandered over to Derek's yard. The cows escaped a lot less with the Ruperts gone, but they still had skills to rival Houdini.

Unbelievably, Mrs. Rupert had kept loosening the fence in hopes the cows would destroy their orchard. When they hadn't, she'd started the fire. Since then, it had occurred to me that maybe Minnie helped them get loose just so she had an excuse to visit her neighbors.

I pulled up in front of my house and Tinker bounded around the corner, going as fast as her legs could carry her, and I braced for impact. She leapt at me, and as she landed against my chest, I lost my balance. I quickly met the ground with a thud.

The breath left me in one whoosh and Tinker

licked my face. Pain radiated from my pelvis and up my back. One of these days, I was going to break my tailbone. After a moment, I was able to sit up.

"Tinker, you know better than that," I said as I stroked her brow. "Seriously. I'm getting too old for this."

I slowly staggered to my feet and took a couple of steps. Tinker whined and nudged my hand with her snout, which was her way of apologizing.

"Just don't do it again," I muttered.

Before I went into the house, I glanced over at Derek's. He and Minnie still stood in his yard, chatting away. Derek waved and as I raised my hand, I realized it was bleeding and I had rocks embedded in my palm.

With a sigh, I opened the front door and headed into the kitchen to clean my hand and take some pain relievers for my back. An hour later, I sat on the couch sandwiched between Tinker and Belle watching re-runs of Friends while drinking hot tea.

"It's going to be an early one for me tonight, girls," I said with a yawn. "Mama is going to get really busy the next couple of weeks and I need my rest."

But yet, I couldn't bring myself to actually head up the stairs. Instead, I had to deal with Derek or I'd never get any sleep.

I grabbed my phone from the coffee table and typed a quick text, then set it back down. My concentration on the show had left the building the minute I hit send, but thankfully, I knew Ross and Rachel were on a break and how the episode ended.

When a knock sounded at the front door, I sighed and stood, then walked over to it. The pain reliever had helped, but I still had some aches in my back end.

I opened the door. Derek stood on my porch wrapped in a thick jacket, his teeth chattering while the wind blew.

"Hi," I said, wishing I had some sparkling conversation to open with.

"Can I come in? It's freezing out here."

"Yes. Sorry. Of course."

He followed me into the kitchen and took off his jacket, then hung it over the back of one of the chairs.

"Do you want some tea?" I asked.

"No, thanks. What's up?"

The dynamic between us had shifted. There used to be a certain electricity that sizzled just beneath the surface and it was no longer there. Nor was the sparkle in his eye as he stared at me expectantly, or the little smile that gave me goosebumps.

"I'm sorry I didn't come see you and that I asked you to come here," I said.

"It's fine, Tilly. I actually have plans for the evening, so I can't stay long. What do you need?"

Plans. He had plans that didn't involve me. And why should they after the way I'd bolted? I'd been so immature—creeping up on forty years of age and I acted like a teen.

"I don't want to keep you if you have plans," I said. "I can talk to you tomorrow."

Derek rolled his eyes and sat down at the kitchen table. "Tilly, I walked over here because you asked me to, and now you're basically telling me to leave. That seems a little ridiculous, don't you think?"

"Yes," I said with a sigh as I gingerly sat down across from him. "It's just downright stupid. I need to talk to you."

"Okay. Go ahead and talk."

My cheeks burned with embarrassment and my words tripped up on my tongue. I tried to find a way to be eloquent, but it wouldn't happen.

"When I was married before and Tommy left me, it was completely awful and destroyed my self-esteem," I blurted. "I thought our relationship was solid. I thought we would be together forever. I never even saw the problems coming until one day, he came home, and instead of eating the meatloaf I made, he told me he was leaving me for a waitress in Little River. Can you imagine that? I was looking forward to a nice dinner and watching some television, and instead, my husband moved out. And to make everything twice as bad, he'd gotten her pregnant."

"Tilly, I—"

"Here's the thing, Derek." I interrupted, unable to meet his gaze or stop my stream of thought. "I'm feeling better about myself, but I'm still scared of getting hurt. When you said you wanted to date me, I told you I needed to take it slow. And we have. But you freaked me out last night when you said you wanted me to kiss you."

"You did bolt from the car pretty quick."

"I know, and I'm embarrassed about that. I just wanted to let you know that my hesitancy doesn't have anything to do with you. It's me. It's up here."

As I tapped my head, I glanced up at him. Relief flood through me when I saw his features had softened.

"I'm sorry he did that to you," he said, his voice quiet. "But I'm not him, Tilly. I like you. A lot. I love spending time with you. Sometimes I want to kiss you so bad, my chest hurts."

He stood and rounded the table. After taking my hand in his, he pulled me to my feet. I winced as pain shot through my back.

"What happened?" he asked.

"Tinker got a little too enthusiastic when she greeted me tonight. I ended up flat on my back in the driveway."

He chuckled as he ran his palm down my cheek. "You sure you're okay?"

"Yes."

Good Lord above, my heart felt like it would beat out the front of my chest. We stood inches apart, and I knew what came next.

"Can I kiss you Tilly?"

His breath whispered across my face, the scent of mints engulfing me. I stood on the proverbial precipice of a tall cliff, and my answer would send me sailing into the unknown. My whole body trembled with excitement and terror.

I had to trust Derek with my heart and hope that he was different from what Tommy had been.

"Yes," I whispered. "But just so you know, I don't make meatloaf anymore."

8

———

THANK GOODNESS FOR GOOGLE MAPS. If I had been looking for Sophia Martinez's house before technology, I never would have found it. She and Jake lived deep in the forest down a bumpy dirt road. Color me surprised when Big Foot didn't dart out in front of my car.

I listened to the directions my phone gave—thankful it still worked out in the middle of nowhere—but my mind was set firmly on that wonderful kiss Derek had laid on me the previous evening. Soft, yet passionate, it left me wanting more. However, that wasn't meant to be the previous night as he was meeting a friend down at the bar and couldn't back out. I felt much more secure since laying out my fears to him, and I looked forward to seeing where our relationship led. I didn't want to fight my attraction to him any longer.

As I pulled up in front of the brown house with blue trim, I glanced around the area. It was as if they'd cleared a few trees and dropped the building. Located between Cedarville and Little River, which was the north point of the Tri-Town area, I imagined they got quite a bit of snow during the winter. The road would be horrible unless they had it plowed. Even then, it would be a muddy mess.

"At least I don't have to deal with it," I muttered as I exited my truck and walked up to the front door.

I had two goals for my visit: Yes, I needed to write some articles for work, but I was also terribly curious about José's threats to Jake. Could he have killed for love? Or worse, could Sophia? We needed to find someone else for the sheriff to focus on besides Carla. I had no intention of throwing anyone under the bus, but José's threats had to be investigated.

I knocked, but no one answered. The wind rustled through the pines as I glanced around. Honestly, the house reminded me of something out of a horror movie. Even more isolated and quiet than my own, it gave me the heebie-jeebies.

After pounding on the door again, I heard footsteps, then Sophia opened the panel.

"Hi!" she said, her brown eyes wide with surprise. "What are you doing here?"

Her long, black hair had been pulled up into a bun and she wore sweats and a long-sleeved T-shirt.

"Hey, Sophia. My name's Tilly Bordeaux. I helped you out at the restaurant the other night."

"I remember."

"Well, I'm also the reporter for the Tri-Town Times, and I was wondering if I could take a few minutes of your time. I'd like to write an article on your dad and the history of Martinez's Mexican Fiesta."

She glanced over her shoulder, then back at me. "I... I guess so."

I stepped inside and she motioned me to the right. The hallway opened up into a living room decorated in seafoam green and yellow. The furniture, littered with cardboard boxes, seemed fairly new. A kitchen sat to the left with bright, shiny stainless steel appliances. I'd considered changing out my appliances when I redid my house a few months ago, and the stainless steel had been incredibly expensive. The ones in the Martinez house also appeared very new.

"Have a seat," she said, removing a couple of the boxes. We sat on the same couch, her on one end and me on the other. I twisted my body to face her.

"Are you moving?" I asked, motioning to the boxes.

"No. Just packing away some things. My dad's stuff."

She certainly wasn't wasting any time. It had been a little more than a week since the murder. Perhaps she felt out of sight, out of mind was the way to go.

"Your house is really nice," I said, glancing around. "The kitchen is really pretty. I love the appliances."

"Oh, thanks," she said with a grin. "I just had them delivered a couple of days ago."

Huh. If my father had been murdered, the last thing I'd do is buy a new refrigerator, but people mourned in different ways. Perhaps Sophia went on a spending spree to attempt to relieve her pain like I'd dive into a box of cookies to alleviate mine.

"Well, I'm sorry about your father," I said. "Like I mentioned, I wanted to do a couple pieces for the paper on him and the restaurant."

"Sure. I understand."

"Can you tell me about your dad? Where he was born? How long did he have the restaurant?"

Sophia nodded and pursed her lips together before speaking. "He came from Mexico when he was a boy and moved to California. His parents were illegal when they crossed the border, but they paid their dues and got their citizenship. He met my mom down in Los Angeles. They married, had me, and then we moved here when I was ten."

I jotted everything down on my notepad, surprised she mentioned her mother. I hadn't heard Carla ever say anything about a Mrs. Martinez, but then again, the Martinezes weren't high on our list of people to discuss. "Where's your mom?"

"She died three years ago."

"Oh, my goodness! I'm so sorry to hear that, Sophia."

The girl shrugged as if it weren't any big deal to lose both parents within such a short period of time, but she said nothing further on that subject.

"Do you have any siblings?"

"No. It's just me."

"Tell me about your dad. Are the recipes made in the restaurant today from him? If so, where did he learn to cook?"

"He was the chef, until he hired José. My abuela,

my grandma, grew her own spices and taught him how to use them. She used to say that everything that went on a plate needed to be fresh—the vegetables, the protein, the tortillas, and especially the spices. That's how you get the amazing flavor and why our restaurant is so popular."

"Where did your grandma learn to cook?"

"I'm not sure, but she was a chef in a Mexican restaurant in Los Angeles. She used to say my dad had a natural ability in the kitchen, and he liked to learn from her when he was growing up."

"And how long ago did he start the restaurant? Was it right when you moved here?"

Sophia nodded. "Yes."

"When did you begin working there?"

"The day I turned sixteen, dad had me waiting tables. Before that, I would help out in the kitchen, but not get paid."

"So he gave you a paycheck at sixteen?"

"Yes."

"Do you like working at the restaurant?"

I hoped so, because she now owned it, according to Carla.

"I do," she said as a smile spread over her face and her cheeks turned crimson. "Once I learn the bookkeeping and everything that Carla is teaching me, I'm really excited to run it."

Based on the way her cheeks flushed, Sophia wasn't excited about being in charge at the restaurant. I had a feeling it was José who put the sparkle in her eye.

"I assume you'll be keeping José around?" I ventured.

She furrowed her brow. "Of course, why?"

"I just saw the way he looked at you," I said with a shrug. "He likes you quite a bit. I assumed you would. He also makes some of the best food in the Tri-Town area."

Her blush deepened and I knew I had my opening.

"Did he and your dad get along?"

"They did," she said with a sigh. "I think my dad saw José as the son he always wished he had. Then they had an argument."

"They liked each other... and then they didn't?"

I knew the answer, but I wanted to see how much she'd tell.

"Not when my dad found out we were dating."

"Why not? I thought he liked José?"

"My dad said he wasn't good enough for me," she

said. "But I'm eighteen and I decided who's good for me and who isn't. José is amazing and we're in love."

"He's quite a bit older than you," I noted. "That's probably why your dad didn't like him."

"Maybe. My dad could be a real jerk sometimes. I knew he didn't want to be in the kitchen anymore. He'd complained about it for years, and he'd been thrilled when he'd hired José because he had the same philosophies as my dad. Everything fresh. But when my dad found out we were dating, he became so rude to José, and José stayed because I asked him to. He'd do anything for me."

"Did José and your dad argue frequently?" I asked.

"My dad would push him with snide remarks, say things about the food he prepared that weren't true... stuff like that. There's only so much a person can take before they blow their top. So, I guess the answer is, yes, they argued frequently, and it was all because my dad didn't want us to date."

"I'm sure that was incredibly stressful."

"It was," she said as she fiddled with her bun. "I'm sorry my dad is dead, but at the same time, it's kind of a relief, you know?"

I stared at her, stunned. Was she that cold, or was her relationship with him so damaged that his death had truly been a reprieve? Or perhaps with her mother dying three years prior, she'd learned to insulate herself from the pain?

"What about your relationship with your dad?" I asked. "Were you close?"

"Not in the past year or so. We were after my mother died, but he sort of just shut down. It was like everything was an irritation to him, especially me and my relationship with José."

"Did José and your father ever come to blows?"

"No. It got close a couple of times. Both he and José said things they didn't mean."

"Like what? Can you give me an example?"

She glanced around the room for a moment, then back at me. "I don't remember."

But she did. I could see it in her face. She was a horrible liar. The fighting went far beyond Jake making nasty remarks about José's cooking.

"I thought you wanted to talk about the restaurant?" Sophia asked. "What does my relationship with José have to do with that?"

"Of course. I guess we got off track there for a minute. Tell me about your plans for the restaurant."

"Ugh. I don't know. Carla says Dad owed everyone money and we're going to have a hard time getting out of the hole. What I'd like to do is revamp the menu and put some of José's dishes on it. Right now it's all my father's recipes. I kind of want to make the restaurant my own, you know what I mean? Maybe add a taco truck so we can get more business than just the restaurant, especially during the lunchtime hours."

I nodded as I jotted down some notes, my thoughts spinning. Perhaps José and Sophia hadn't seen Jake's hatred of their relationship coming. If Jake had made their lives miserable enough, perhaps they had poisoned him. Without him around, Sophia was ready to take the restaurant in a different direction, and from the sound of her plans, José would be there with her every step of the way. They both won with Jake's loss.

Carla had said she'd heard José threaten to kill Jake, and there hadn't been any reason for her to lie, unless she'd murdered him herself and needed to place blame somewhere else, which I didn't believe for a hot second.

"Has the sheriff mentioned any suspects to you?" I asked as nonchalantly as possible. I found it difficult to believe Sophia would keep employing Carla if she knew my friend was the focus of the investigation.

"No. Nothing. Have you heard anything about who may be responsible for killing my father?"

I shook my head and didn't meet her gaze. "Nope. I assume our good sheriff would come to you first."

"He hasn't said anything," she said with a shrug.

"Well, that's all the questions I have," I said as I stood. "Thank you so much for your time, Sophia. Again, I'm sorry for your loss."

As she walked me to the door and we said our goodbyes, I wondered about her and José. Could an eighteen-year-old girl be callous enough to kill her own father because he didn't like who she was dating? Could her boyfriend be frustrated enough to murder her father?

Two things were certain: it sure seemed like both of their lives were a lot easier without Jake, and I needed to talk to José... alone.

9

———

WHEN I ARRIVED home from Sophia's, I caught Tinker when she lunged at me and managed to wrestle her down. I really should have taken her to puppy school before she had grown into her full weight. Maybe she'd have some manners and be less of a challenge when she was excited.

"Let's go feed your chickens," I said as I patted her pretty brow. "How are they today?"

Tinker raced ahead of me as I rounded the house. I found her standing next to the chicken coop, wagging her tail.

I'd named the chickens Butter and Batter, but I didn't tell anyone. It was my own personal joke that may offend some people. I had no intention of buttering or battering either hen, but I gave myself a chuckle when I said hello to them.

Once I'd gathered their feeder, I took it to the spigot on the side of the house to rinse it out. I heard them clucking, and I could almost decipher what they said: Hurry up! The chickens and I had not bonded, but I kept them around because I liked the eggs and Tinker would be devastated if I got rid of her friends. If my dog was in love with the chickens, there was no way I would destroy that for her. Anything for my Tinker.

I went to the garage and retrieved their food. As I returned to the coop, I studied the planters that should have held some crops this past summer, but I'd been too busy to plant them. I love fresh vegetables, and promised myself I'd get around to it in the spring.

"Here you go, you vicious beasts," I said as I placed the feeder back into the pen. I watched them as they ate, acting like they hadn't had a scrap of food in days.

I headed back to the house and saw Derek coming my way. He waved and my heart fluttered while I waited for him on the porch.

"Hey, neighbor," he said. "I saw your truck drive by and I wanted to come say hello."

"I'm glad you did," I replied, taking a seat on the porch swing. "Did you have fun last night?"

He joined me and we sat shoulder to shoulder. "I did. I drank a couple of sodas and played a few rounds of pool but I would have rather been somewhere else."

"Like where?"

"I kept thinking about this really beautiful woman I know who finally let me kiss her. I wanted to spend time with her instead of at the bar. And perhaps steal another kiss."

A blush crawled over my cheeks as he grabbed my hand, giving it a quick squeeze.

"You're so sweet," I said, unable to meet his gaze. Would I ever get over feeling like a teenage girl around him?

"Tell me about your day, Tilly. What have you been up to?"

"Ugh. I went to see Sophia Martinez."

"What for?"

"Articles for the paper," I said with a sigh. "Harold has us in high gear again because of the murder. Instead of putting out editions a couple times a month, we're moving to once or twice a week until the murder is solved."

"That should keep you busy and from trying to find out who killed Jake."

I smiled and met his gaze. "It should."

"So tell me what Sophia said."

I reiterated our conversation. "The whole thing was weird, though. It was like she didn't care her father had died. She was already cleaning out his stuff. There were boxes everywhere. She didn't even look upset when we talked about his death. She'd even bought new kitchen appliances. Who does that when their parent dies?"

"People grieve in different ways. Maybe shopping makes her feel better."

"A definite possibility. It just seemed surreal to me."

We sat in silence for a bit, our feet moving in tandem to keep the swing going.

"Do you think she killed Jake?" Derek asked.

"I honestly don't know," I replied, shaking my head. "She wasn't all that upset about him dying. That, I'm sure of."

"A lot of people were talking about the murder at the bar last night."

"Really? What were they saying?"

"Mainly that Jake was not a good guy and there wouldn't be a lot of people missing him."

"What did he do?"

Derek shrugged. "He owed people money. Had some shady business dealings. The IRS has been interested in him for a while. Stuff like that."

"Even his own daughter says he wasn't very nice."

"If all that's true, why did Carla continue to work for him?" Derek asked.

"I have no idea. I've asked her and she said she doesn't want to go back to serving. She wants a management position."

Derek sighed and shook his head. "Well, if things get bad enough, she'll take what she can get."

"Now she's set on teaching Sophia the ropes so she can take over the restaurant."

"Hmm."

"What does that mean?"

"Nothing."

"No, don't nothing me, Derek. What are you thinking?"

"I was just thinking that Sophia... well, perhaps she's like her father. She's just not a nice person."

The sun had begun to set and a thick chill hung in the air. I wouldn't be able to stay outside much longer.

"She seems nice enough," I replied. "She was

sweet when we worked at the restaurant, and she was fine today."

"But you didn't like the fact that she was packing up her father's things and buying new appliances."

"No, that was cold. You have a point. Maybe she is like her father. The apple may not fall far from the tree."

I shivered and Derek put his arm around me. As I rested my head on his shoulder, I appreciated the warmth he offered.

"Do you want to have dinner together?" he asked.

"I was going to have a grilled cheese and some tomato soup. Do you want to join me?"

"I'd love to."

We made our way into the house and I busied myself in the kitchen.

"Let me help you," Derek said, and his offer cracked away at my defenses just a little bit more. My ex-husband liked me to wait on him, and me thinking I was being the excellent wife, I had. Derek, on the other hand, helped me with the sandwiches and stirred the soup.

"I've got warm tea or iced tea," I said as I stared into the refrigerator. "I need to go to the store."

"No worries. I'm fine with water."

In my effort to regain my confidence and lose

weight, I'd also given up soda. I didn't miss it, but I never had any beverage options to offer guests.

I turned around to find him standing in the middle of the kitchen carrying a tray laden with our food. "Do you want to watch some television while we eat?" he asked with a grin.

Did this man's niceties ever end?

With a nod, I followed him into the living room.

The evening passed quickly, and before I knew it, nine o'clock had arrived. Derek gave me a soft kiss goodnight, then left for his own home.

After I shut the door, I leaned against it and sighed. My lips tingled where he'd kissed me and my heart fluttered in my chest.

Warmth spread throughout my body and I couldn't stop smiling.

Good grief. Was I falling in love?

THE NEXT MORNING, I stopped into Debbie's to see what she'd learned. It was always hard keeping up with her schedule beyond work because she went to bed so early to be able get up before the sun and bake her daily sweet offerings.

"Good morning, my friend," she said as I entered, wishing I'd worn a coat. "What's going on?"

I glanced at her customers crowding around their tables, and I was happy to see her so busy. A few people waved to me and I smiled as I approached the counter.

"How are you?" I took the cup of coffee Debbie handed me.

"Fine. Busy."

"You need to hire someone."

"I did. They quit."

We sat down at a table near the register. "Perhaps you're just hard to get along with."

Debbie nodded in agreement. "I'm certain I'm a terrible boss. I have a hard time allowing others to do the work."

"You're afraid they're going to mess everything up?"

"Yes. Apparently, I have trust issues."

"Apparently."

"Things have been quiet on the Jake Martinez front," Debbie said, her gaze shifting all around the store. "No one knows much about him. The guy kind of kept to himself, but I did hear one interesting thing about him."

"What's that?"

"Remember that Mexican restaurant that opened in Little River, but then closed right away?"

"Sure."

"Rumor had it that Jake had something to do with it."

"Like what?"

The door chime rang and a couple of people walked in. I recognized Betty Frank from the Feed store. As she glanced over at me, I waved, but she gave me the side-eye and then ignored me. Last time I had shopped for chicken feed, she had one of her employees wait on me.

The woman wanted nothing to do with me. I had put her best friend in prison for murder, so I understood I wasn't high on her list of favorite people.

Debbie waited on everyone, then returned to the table. "What was I saying?"

"You were about to tell me how Jake had something to do with the Mexican restaurant closing in Little River."

"That's right. Linda works over in the City Hall and knows someone who works in the department that coordinates with the state Health Department. She told me yesterday that the reason the restaurant closed was because someone reported them for unhygienic practices. She couldn't verify it was Jake, but it makes sense."

I frowned. "She thinks Jake turned in his competitor?"

"Yes."

"And what were the unhygienic practices?"

Debbie leaned over the table after glancing around to make sure no one heard us. "They found a dead rat in the sink, as well as rodent feces all over the kitchen, including in the food."

"Eww," I said with a grimace. "That's disgusting."

"But the guy said his place had just been inspected, and it came back with an A+ grade. He thinks he was set up."

"What's his name?"

"Darryl Hill," Debbie replied.

"And he thinks Jake was responsible for the rat and everything else?"

"Yes. The health department shut him down fast."

"Interesting. I never heard about that."

"Darryl Hill also lived and worked in Little River. Although we're called the Tri-Towns, we do keep to our regions of the triangle. Besides, from what I understand, it happened really fast. Everyone was on to the next thing, and that's probably why we never knew the full story."

"I bet that really upset Mr. Hill."

"I can't imagine," Debbie replied with a long sigh. "I wake up at night in cold sweats with nightmares about my place being shut down for health violations."

"Really?'

"Oh, yes. It's high on the list of worries for those who own eating establishments. Cleanliness is truly next to godliness in this business."

"How would Jake plant the rat and the rest of it in the restaurant?"

Debbie shrugged. "Off the top of my head, I would guess he would have had to break in with all that stuff, set it up, then call the inspectors."

Martinez's Mexican Fiesta was open every day. I just assumed the Little River restaurant would have been as well.

"How would he do that?" I asked. "Did the restaurant close a few days during the week?"

"I don't know. Maybe Darryl closed on Mondays or something like that. A lot of restaurants have a day off around here."

"I'm going to ask Sophia about this," I said, rising from the table. "See what she has to say."

"Why?" Debbie asked, also standing. "It's not like it has anything to do with Jake's death. If it's true, it'll prove that Jake's an even bigger jerk than we thought, but that's about it."

"Unless Darryl Hill got so angry at what Jake had done, he had him killed."

Debbie arched an eyebrow and nodded. "There's that theory. It doesn't hold a lot of weight, but it's a possibility."

"We'll see. I know we're grasping at straws here, but you never know. Each day they close in on Carla being arrested. I have to do everything in my power to make sure that doesn't happen. I have to at least try to give them other suspects."

"Carla sure isn't worried about it."

"I know, and it's making me insane. It's like I care about her freedom more than she does. She tells me that she's innocent, so they won't arrest her."

Debbie rolled her eyes. "Like you said, Tilly, the sheriff only cares that he has someone in custody before the election. If he can make the narrative fit, he'll use it."

"I know."

"Good luck, hon," she said, giving me a hug. "Let me know what you turn up."

I HURRIED BACK to the office and sighed with relief when I found it empty. My deadline for the article on Jake was looming, and Harold would wonder where it was. I decided I'd work on it as soon as I called Sophia, but then I realized I didn't have her phone number, only her address. I didn't have time to drive back to Cedarville to see her, so I took the shortest route in getting the digits and called Carla.

Thankfully, she picked up.

"I need Sophia's number," I said. "I need to verify something with her."

Carla hesitated for a moment before answering. "I'm not sure I should give it to you, Tilly."

"Why not?"

"Because if she wanted you to have it, she would have handed it over."

"I never asked for it," I replied as I tossed my pen on the desk in frustration. "This has to do with you possibly not going to jail."

"I'm sorry, but that's confidential work stuff. It's not me giving you the number to the local dry cleaner. It's her personal number."

Gritting my teeth, I tried keep the fury out of my voice. "Can you please break this one damn rule, Carla? I'm trying to save your hide."

"I'm sorry, Tilly," she said with a loud sigh. "I can't. Rules are in place for a reason."

Oh, how I wanted to rattle some common sense into her. "That's fine. You can help me. I was wondering about a problem between Jake and Darryl Hill."

"The guy who owned the place in Little River?"

"Yes."

"What about him?"

I told her the story Debbie had shared.

"A rat? No way. That's just disgusting."

Disappointment railed through me as I rubbed my forehead. "Are you sure?"

"Well, no. But that's just... I don't even know the word for it. Setting up a rival like that? It's cold."

Carla wasn't certain, and that left room for a possibility, but I could see I wouldn't be getting anywhere with her. In fact, my friend was on my very last nerve. "Can you have Sophia call me?"

"Sure. She should be in later today."

I hung up and began my Google search for Darryl Hill. If I didn't find anything on my own, I'd go down to City Hall and look at the licensing records. His restaurant had only been open a few months before it closed, but he had to have a license to operate it.

My internet search became a trip down a rabbit hole, and I finally located him on Facebook. He'd had a page set up for the restaurant. As I scrolled through, I took great interest in the comments.

José was a constant contributor, and he wasn't pleasant, to put it mildly.

Under a picture of fajitas, he wrote, Is that a pile of worms?

When Darryl announced Taco Tuesday with pictures of some ground beef tacos, José wrote, Are you sure you use beef? That looks like rat.

There was more.

This place is unsanitary.

I'd rather take a bullet than eat here.

And under Darryl's last post saying that he was closing down: Adios, Amigo.

I didn't understand why Darryl had kept the insults up on his page. Why hadn't he deleted them? It didn't make any sense.

My phone rang and startled me out of my reverie. I took a few deep breaths before answering Sophia's call.

"Hi, Sophia," I said. "Thanks for getting back to me."

"Sure. What's up?"

I once again told the story I'd heard about the rat in Darryl's restaurant. To my surprise, Sophia broke out into peals of laughter.

"Yeah, that was us."

"So... your dad planted the rat?"

"My dad and José did it, but it was my idea."

I stared at my computer screen, at a complete loss for words and utterly shocked at the pride in her voice. How could an eighteen-year-old girl be so cruel?

Because she had such a jerk for a father. The more I learned about the family, the less sorry I was Jake had lost his life.

And why was she admitting this? Probably

because she was eighteen, immature, and thought the whole situation was terribly amusing.

"Did Darryl Hill know you guys did it?"

"Oh, he suspected it. We also trolled him all over social media."

"Why?"

"Because our business was going down," Sophia said. "People were trying out the new place, and we couldn't have that."

I closed my eyes and bit my bottom lip. So much for friendly competition. "Did Darryl ever say anything to your dad about the rat?"

"Sure he did. He came in here one night all lit up and angrier than a cornered possum."

"What did he say? Did they have a fight?"

"Darryl said my dad better watch his back because he'd get his revenge."

"Did he mention what that revenge looked like?"

"Yes. He said he'd kill him."

AFTER I HUNG up with Sophia, my stomach rolled from disgust at the Martinez's Mexican Fiesta crew, as well as stress over my job. I felt like I was being pulled in fifty different directions. On one hand, I had a job to do, but I didn't seem to be able to sit down and concentrate on the articles. The urge to head to Little River and speak with Darryl Hill tugged at me. Why hadn't he called the police when the harassment started? Why had he left the horrible comment José had posted on his social media? I needed answers, but then again, if he was a killer, I shouldn't be tangling with him. Yet, I had to meet him to get a feel for him. Was he capable of murder?

I had four good suspects to hand over to the police. They had to investigate Sophia and José, the farmer, Jerry, and now Darryl Hill. They thought they had Carla set up perfectly, but they didn't. She may have been the last one to see Jake and fought with him before she left, but she had no reason to kill him. At least none that she shared with me, but then again, she hadn't been very forthcoming with any information this whole time I'd been trying to help her avoid going to prison for a crime she didn't commit.

At least, I hoped she hadn't.

I realized I'd been so surprised by Sophia's admission, I never asked why she didn't call the police when Darryl threatened Jake. When I glanced at my phone, I saw that I had her number from our previous conversation. She picked up right away when I pressed the dial button.

"Did you tell the police about Darryl's threat?"

"No, we didn't," she replied. "If we had, we'd have had to admit what we'd done, so I just let it go. Besides, my dad would never let him in his house or the restaurant. They're saying my dad was poisoned, which meant someone had to give it to him."

"You don't think it's a possibility that he snuck into your house or the restaurant?"

"Everything was alarmed. There's just no way in without us knowing."

"Okay, thanks, Sophia. I appreciate your help."

As I set down my phone, I recalled when I'd gone into Martinez's Mexican Restaurant with Carla that morning we'd found Jake. No alarm had sounded and Carla hadn't mentioned it. Perhaps it was a silent alarm, so she didn't think anything of it? Or maybe she knew the alarm wasn't going to go off because when she'd killed Jake, she'd left and didn't turn it on.

"She's innocent," I said to my empty office. I couldn't allow myself to travel down that path of thinking that she was anything else.

But honestly, when I looked at the facts, I understood why the police had their sights set on her. Her actions made her look guilty, as well as the fact she'd changed her story of what had happened that night.

I sighed and pulled out my laptop. First things first. I had to get my articles written.

An hour later, I had one completed about Jake Martinez and his history, and I began one on the restaurant. It made me sick to write such niceties when I knew the truth about the murdered man and his family. Yet, I couldn't print any of the horrible things they'd done unless I could corroborate it with Darryl Hill. But then again, did I want to drag a dead man through the mud for a story? Did any of it really matter at this point? I may not like Sophia, but to write on the deceitful practices of her father didn't sit well with me. He was dead, and somewhere in that cold heart of hers, I had to assume she was hurting.

Harold entered the building like his butt had caught on fire, and I practically jumped out of my chair.

"Tilly! I'm glad you're here," he said as he dumped his computer bag on his desk. "You'll never guess where I've been."

A satisfied smile crept over his face as he crossed his arms over his chest. The cat who ate the canary or the old-school, hard-hitting editor who'd just landed a whale-sized story.

"I can't imagine, Harold," I said, sitting back in my chair and preparing for the big reveal. "Tell me. I know it's something good."

"I've been having lunch with Doctor Wheeler."

"And?"

"And he's expecting the results from toxicology soon. We'll know exactly what poison killed Jake Martinez. He's going to call us first."

"Even before he calls Sophia?" I said, arching my brows. "I would think he'd notify the family before the paper."

"Of course, of course," Harold said as he walked around his desk and sat down. "My point being, we don't have to wait to hear it from the police."

"Ah, I see," I replied. What he hadn't said was that I'd pretty much burned the fragile bridge between us and the sheriff's office. They most likely wouldn't be very cooperative.

I didn't know anything about poisons, so I was curious to see what Doctor Wheeler had to say.

"This article is good," Harold said as he stared at his computer. "Nice work, Tilly. I was beginning to worry that you'd lost your touch."

"No, just really busy," I said.

"With what? You aren't trying to hunt down a killer, are you?"

"Of course not," I said with a smile. "That would be dangerous and stupid."

"I'm glad to hear you say that. Sometimes I worry that you get yourself in over your head."

"Sometimes, I do," I replied and returned my focus to my computer.

For now, I had to think about my next step. Did I call Byron and tell him what I know, or go visit Darryl Hill, a potential murderer, in Little River?

11

"How do you figure you have four suspects?" Debbie asked.

We sat at my kitchen table putting together a jigsaw puzzle while rain poured outside. It was a picture of old soda bottles and we weren't making much progress. I had too much on my mind to concentrate.

"Sophia and José... they're crazier than a three-headed pig," I said as I picked up a puzzle piece, then set it back down.

Debbie shook her head and clucked her tongue. "They definitely seem to be a few wires short upstairs."

"If I'm going with the theory that they killed Jake,

I don't know whether to think that they did it separately or together."

"I think they did it together," Debbie said as she snapped a piece into place. "Crazy loves crazy, Tilly."

"I know. I can't help but wonder about Darryl Hill. If it had been my restaurant, I'd be mad enough to kill."

"You and me both."

"But I feel like I've got to talk to him about the situation. I'm getting one side."

"Yes, but Sophia admitted to their guilt. She, José, and Jake were thick as thieves in that one."

"I know. I just don't understand why she didn't tell Sheriff Connor about the threat. The man said he'd kill Jake."

"Because she would have to admit her own wrongdoing at the time, as well as her father's and José's. It was easier to let it slide. Besides, from what you've told me, she doesn't seem too broken up about her father's death anyway. In fact, it solved a problem for her and paved the way for smooth sailing. She's got her boyfriend and she's got her restaurant. I think she did it."

"Do you really think an eighteen-year-old girl is capable of killing her father?" I asked.

"A black, ugly heart of evil," Debbie replied. "Besides, she has to have heard that the Sheriff believes Carla committed the murder, and Sophia still keeps her around. That's weird to me. She obviously doesn't think Carla did it, and that's because she knows in her soul who killed him."

"I don't think the sheriff has let anyone know his suspicions," I said. "The only reason I'm aware is because Byron let it slip when he took my statement."

"Okay, whatever," Debbie said, then took a sip of tea. "But trust me, that girl is wicked."

"I don't know, Debbie," I said, picking up another piece of the puzzle and twirling it around in my fingers. "What about the farmer? Jerry? He definitely could have done it."

"The guy Jake owed money to?"

"Yes."

"He's a good possibility as well, especially after what he said. Did he mean that he hoped he'd get paid by Sophia if Jake was dead, or that he thought Sophia would be a better business partner than Jake had been?"

"I just feel like I'm missing something," I said with a sigh.

"Well, remember... we aren't supposed to be solving this murder. Just give the police another place to hang their hat besides on Carla."

I groaned when my doorbell rang. Even though I had been the one to invite Byron over, I knew he'd be upset with me about the topic of conversation.

"Thanks again for being here for this," I said to Debbie, then stood.

"Sure, hon. I'm always here for you."

I'd invited Debbie over to act as a barrier between Byron and me. I hoped it would prevent any conversation about our non-existent relationship as well as my budding romance with Derek.

When I opened the door, Byron's gaze settled on me for a second, then went over my shoulder as if he searched for something... or someone.

"What's up, Tilly?"

"I was hoping you and I could talk for a few minutes."

"Sure."

I led him into the kitchen and his shoulders sagged when he saw Debbie. Perhaps he thought he'd find someone else? Like Derek?

"Hey, Debbie," he said with a grin, obviously pleased to see her.

"Byron. How's your day been?"

"Fine," he said as he sat down at the table. "What can I do for you ladies?"

I took my chair and cleared my throat. "I need to talk to you about Jake Martinez's death."

Byron rolled his eyes. "Tilly, I told you to stay out of it."

"I know, and I am. Truly. I just want you to listen for a minute."

He crossed his arms over his chest and glared at me. "Fine. Go ahead."

"Well, I think there are some other people who should be investigated besides Carla."

"You've said this before."

"I know, but please just listen to what I've discovered."

He stared intently at me as I laid out my suspects. Each had far more reason to kill Jake than Carla.

"You really think a young girl is going to have the stomach to kill her own father?" he asked. "You're out of your mind."

"No, she's not," Debbie interjected. "It's a possibility, and it needs to be looked into, Byron."

"Carla has motive," he countered, holding up his hand. He pushed one finger down. "She and Jake argued before she left that night." Another finger went down. "She lied about that." Another one. "Poisoning is typically a woman's weapon. Men usually kill with more force. A bullet. A knife. Carla said that—"

"Sharon Rupert killed Mr. York with a knife," I interrupted. "So I get your theory, but it was just proved that women are perfectly capable of killing up close and personal with force."

Byron glared at me once again, his lips pursed together, but at least he'd put his hand back in his lap.

"So you think Carla just happened to have some poison in her purse?" I asked.

"It's a possibility," Byron said with a shrug. "She'd decided she'd either get the raise, or Jake would die."

"Wouldn't that be premeditated murder?" I asked.

"Yes."

"Have you searched her home? Her purse?"

"I can't comment on that, Tilly."

With a grunt, I slammed my hand down on the table in frustration, which only made my finger I'd smashed in the door hurt worse.

"All we're saying is that these other people have

to be looked at before Carla is arrested," Debbie said. "We know she didn't do it."

"You don't know," Byron replied. "You want it to be true because she's your friend, but you have absolutely no evidence to back up your feelings."

As I stared at my fingernail that had turned black, I realized he had a valid point. Carla had been distant since the murder and didn't seem very concerned that the sheriff had her in his crosshairs. Touching base with her to find out what was going on with her case was more difficult than getting a politician to be truthful.

Maybe she felt guilty about what she'd done and was ready to go away for it.

"Are we finished here?" Byron asked.

"I guess so," I said. "I was just hoping you'd look at the other people I mentioned."

Byron stood, his chair scraping against the tile. "I'll run it by the sheriff."

I followed him to the front door.

"Will you step outside with me?" he asked, his voice quiet.

"What's up?" I asked before closing the door behind me. The sun had set and the cold air gave me goosebumps, even though I wore a long-sleeved shirt.

"Are you still seeing that druggie?"

I sighed as my anger heated me from within. "He's not a druggie, Byron. He had some problems in his youth but has straightened himself out."

Lightning cracked and lit up his face for a brief second. His brow furrowed in fury, he fisted his hands at his sides.

"Once a druggie, always a druggie, Tilly. Trust me on that."

"It's really none of your business who I'm seeing," I said through gritted teeth. "Is there anything else?"

Another bolt cracked in the sky. Byron's features softened and I swore his eyes teared up just a bit before he glanced over at Derek's house. "I just don't understand what happened between us. I thought we got along really well."

Ah, yes... the one conversation I had desperately wanted to avoid. How did I tell him that he bored me, that I found him nice to look at, but his head was emptier than an abandoned dumpster?

I didn't. I wouldn't hurt him that way.

"Byron, it's not you. It's me."

Regret coursed through me as the words hit the space between us and I tried to backtrack to save myself. "What I mean is, when you asked me out, I'd just gotten divorced. I should have said no. I wasn't in a good place mentally."

"And now? What about now?"

I glanced over at Derek's house. Yes, I was in a better place, and some of that had to do with my budding relationship with Derek, but most of it had to do with me feeling a lot better about myself. I excelled at my job and I had wonderful friends. I'd lost weight. I'd made my house mine and erased Tommy from it. So yes, things were looking up, but that didn't mean I wanted to date Byron.

"I'm doing well," I said, deciding to be honest. "It's just not going to work between us."

He nodded and crossed his arms over his chest. "This hurts, Tilly."

"I'm sorry to upset you," I said, laying my hand on his forearm. "I don't want to do that."

A gust of wind whipped across my porch and sent a chill down my spine. I needed to wrap this up.

"I hope we can still be friends, Byron. There's no reason why we can't spend time together in that capacity."

He nodded and stepped off the porch. Just as I was about to head inside, he turned around. "Are the chickens okay?"

"They're fine. Tinker is still having her love affair with them."

Byron glanced around my driveaway as the rain pelted him. It reminded me of a romantic movie where the woman had just broken the man's heart and he walked away in the downpouring rain, his will to live gone.

Finally, he looked back at me. "Take care, Tilly."

"You too," I replied. "I'll see you around, and feel free to stop by anytime."

As soon as he slid into the patrol vehicle, I went back inside, feeling terrible. At least I had been more honest and nicer to him than Tommy had been with me during our separation.

"It's so cold out there," I said, my teeth chattering.

"Winter is coming," Debbie said, her voice ominous. "Almost time for me to break out the peppermint coffee and caramel donuts."

"I hope we don't get too much snow."

"You and me both, Tilly. You and me both."

I picked up another puzzle piece and studied what we'd accomplished. I tried it in a couple different places, and finally snapped it in. Even though it was only one piece, I raised my hands in triumph.

My thoughts returned to my conversation with

Byron. If he was only going to pass my theories on to the sheriff instead of actually investigating them, chances were good they'd be ignored. I needed to follow up with some of my suspects. I could do that under the guise of being a reporter, but I may be confronting a murderer, which was dangerous business.

12

THE NEXT MORNING, I stood at my kitchen sink gulping down a quick cup of coffee and holding Belle when I saw Derek walking from his house to mine carrying a box I recognized as one from Debbie's Deliciousness.

"Oh, my word, Belly-Belle," I murmured as I stroked her head. "That man has brought us donuts. He keeps getting better and better at this dating stuff. Before long, I'm going to think he's perfect."

She swished her tail and meowed.

"Let's go see. I just hope they're sugar-free."

I opened the door as he bounded up the steps. "Good morning!"

"Hey, Tilly," he said, his face breaking into a large

smile. "I was hoping you'd have time to have breakfast with me."

The way he stared at me curled my toes. It was as if I had become the most important person in his life and he couldn't wait to be with me.

"I have a few minutes," I replied, stepping aside and allowing him to pass. "That's really sweet of you. Thank you."

As I followed him to the kitchen, I set Belle down. She immediately began weaving in and out of his legs and he handled it like a pro—barely a misstep.

He sat down at the kitchen table and Tinker burst through her dog door and over to Derek, her tail wagging a million miles an hour.

"Hey, girl!" he said, scratching behind her ears. "I'm glad to see you, too."

I poured two cups of coffee and joined him.

"Debbie said you like sugar-free." He opened the box.

"That's true. Thank you. Have you had these? The strawberry is amazing."

I pulled one out and set it on a napkin in front of me.

"Debbie said those were your favorites."

I groaned after taking a bite, then covered my

mouth with my hand. "It sounds like you and Debbie are in cahoots."

"Just want to make sure I got you the right donuts," Derek said as he ate. "These are good."

We sat in silence for a few moments while we devoured the deliciousness.

"So, what's on your agenda today?" he asked as he sat back in his chair and took a sip of coffee.

"I'm going up to Little River for a few hours, but then I'll be back at the office this afternoon."

"What's in Little River?"

"I'm writing an article on Martinez's Mexican Fiesta. There's someone up there I need to interview."

I rose from the table and went to the refrigerator to get the cream for my coffee while hoping he didn't ask me any further questions. I didn't want to lie, but I also knew he wouldn't approve that I was planning to see Darryl Hill, the owner of the Mexican restaurant Jake had shut down for health violations. I'd tried to call, but the only number I'd been able to find had been out of service.

There was no way for me to tie him to a story except through Jake's murder, and Derek cared enough to not want me investigating that.

"What are you doing today?" I asked, hoping to change the subject. "Anything exciting?"

"Actually, yes," he said as I sat down.

"What's that?"

"Well, first, there's going to be a little ceremony at the school. I bought them new instruments for the band class, and they're going to be playing for me today."

I stared at him a beat, shocked to my core. His well of generosity shouldn't surprise me, but it did. In the past few months, he'd also purchased computers for the library, blankets for the homeless shelter, and spent a few evenings reading to the kids who lived there. I admired that he sat on a stack of cash and wanted to help others.

His kindness actually brought tears to my eyes.

"Why are you crying?" He reached for my hand, his blue gaze shining with concern.

"You're the nicest person," I replied as the tears fell and I wiped them away.

"Not always, Tilly," he whispered. "When I was on drugs, I did some horrible things. I guess I'm trying to atone for my behavior back then."

We hadn't really discussed his past in great detail. I knew he'd stolen from his parents and his father, Mr. York, had said that the stress of his addiction had killed Derek's mother. But besides that, I knew nothing.

The life of a drug addict was completely foreign to me. Did I want to know the horrible things he'd done, or would it only taint my growing appreciation of him?

People were not perfect, and the world was not made up of black and white. Shades of gray lay everywhere and people could change.

"Perhaps sometime you can tell me about your past... what your life was like when you were on drugs."

Derek took a sip of his coffee before answering. "I don't know if that's something I want to share with you. It wasn't pretty."

"I'm sure it wasn't, but I think we should discuss it."

"You're probably right," he replied with a sigh. "But not now."

"No, definitely not now. What's the other thing you're going to do?"

"Well, I bought the orchard next door, and I'm having the land razed."

This stunned me more than his generous gift to the band club.

The orchard had burned down about five

months ago and the owner, Bill Rupert, had simply disappeared.

"Did the property go into foreclosure?"

"It did. I've had my attorney watching for that, and I scooped it up. I don't know about you, but I'm tired of looking at those black, mangled trees."

"Oh, goodness, yes! The orchard was so beautiful, especially when the trees were in bloom. I miss them."

"Why don't you think about what you would like to see over there?"

"Are you going to keep the property?"

"I don't know. I could turn it and make a profit, but I'd also like to have some control over what's done with it. I don't think we need any more cows with incredible escape skills around."

"Agreed," I said with a laugh.

We finished our coffee in comfortable silence, then I glanced at the clock. "I really need to get going."

"Of course," he said, quickly standing and grabbing both of our coffee cups, then hurrying over to the sink.

We walked out the front door together, and I said goodbye to Tinker and Belle before shutting it.

"Have a great day, Tilly," he said, running his hands over my arms.

My heartrate quickened. Was it his touch or all the coffee I'd consumed? "You, too."

Butterflies tickled my belly and heat rushed into my cheeks.

"Can I give you a kiss?"

"I'd really like that," I whispered.

As his lips met mine, I couldn't think of a more perfect way to start my day.

THE DRIVE to Little River went smoothly--very little traffic and no road construction, which surprised me. It seemed like they always had that stretch of highway torn up for some reason or another.

I tried to breathe through the nervous energy coursing through me. My ex lived in Little River, and although chances were slim I'd actually run into him, I worried I would. We weren't exactly friendly after our last conversation when I'd told him to come get his stuff or I was donating it to Goodwill. He'd never showed, and I'd followed through on my promise. I just didn't want any confrontation with him to ruin my day.

I'd found Darryl Hill's address through Google, and when I pulled up in front of the closed Mexican restaurant, Cantina Mexicana, I sat in the car staring at the abandoned building.

"What the heck?" I murmured. "Did I drive all the way up here for the wrong address?"

I pulled out my phone and looked it up again. The almighty Google told me that Darryl Hill lived there, in apartment number two.

"Maybe Google is wrong."

While debating whether or not to drive back home or knock on the front door of the abandoned building, I saw a man walk around from the back of the restaurant and over to two mailboxes by the sidewalk that I hadn't noticed before.

Was there an apartment behind the main structure?

I pushed the drive gear into park and slid out of my truck. A few papers fell to the pavement, and I reached down and grabbed them, then threw them back into the truck. I really needed to clean it out. The man had gathered his mail and was walking the way he'd come.

"Excuse me!" I said, breaking into a jog.

He glanced over at me and waited.

"What can I do for you?"

"Hi," I said, surprised I wasn't completely out of breath. Exercise really wasn't my thing. "My name's Tilly Bordeaux with the Tri-Town Times. I'm looking for Darryl Hill."

"That's me," he said, his brow furrowing in curiosity. "What's this about?"

I pegged him to be in his forties, tall, and so bald, except for the black mustache, I wondered if he'd ever had hair. "I wanted to ask you a couple of questions about Jake Martinez and his restaurant."

He pursed his lips and crossed his arms over his chest. I could feel the anger simmering just beneath the surface. "What about him?"

"I assume you know he's dead?"

A slow smile spread across his face. "Oh, yeah. I think I read about it... last week or so?"

"Yes."

"Best day of my life."

I nodded, fully understanding his joy. "I heard what he did to you."

"Put me right out of business," Darryl grumbled, pointing at the restaurant. "Had me shut down."

"Yes, I know."

"As far as I'm concerned, the jerk got what was coming to him."

"I've been hearing that a lot."

"Who drowns a rat because he can't handle the competition?" Darryl said, shaking his head. "Disgusting behavior."

"Did he admit he did that?" I asked.

"Oh, yeah. I confronted him about it. He fully copped to it without saying a word."

"And how did he do that?"

"He laughed. Just laughed like destroying a man's livelihood was the funniest thing he'd ever done. He was guilty."

A burst of wind blew, and I thought I felt a couple of raindrops fall from the gray sky as my hair whipped my face. "I looked at your Facebook page, Mr. Hill. There were so many negative comments from José. Why didn't you block him, or delete them?"

"Oh, believe me, I tried," Darryl replied. "At first, I had no idea who he was, but after asking around a bit, I figured out he worked for Jake. It seemed like I couldn't delete his comments fast enough. Couldn't figure out how to block him, though. I'm not real good with the computer, and that social media... well, I think it's just stupid."

"Why did you have an account then?"

"One of my servers said I needed one to get the word out about the restaurant."

"I see."

Social media had become an intricate part of most people's lives.

"Why are you asking me about Jake and his restaurant?" Darryl asked.

Now came the tricky part. I didn't want to make it seem as if I was accusing him of murder, but I had to get a read on his threat. Had it been empty, or had he meant it?

"Jake's daughter, Sophia, told me you threatened to kill Jake."

"I sure did."

"Well, he was murdered."

"Can't say I'm sorry to hear that. Are you asking me if I did it?"

I shrugged and tucked a lock of hair behind my ear. "It crossed my mind."

Darryl laughed and shook his head. "I didn't kill Jake. I would have liked to wrap my hands around his neck and squeeze the life out of him after what he pulled, but I never did."

Did I believe him? As I studied his face, I thought I saw truth there, but I couldn't be sure. Was he admitting to the threat, but trying to cover up the crime?

"Are you going to open up your restaurant again?" I asked.

"Maybe. Haven't decided. Don't know if the state will even allow me to."

I glanced over at the building again, feeling bad for the man. "Well, if you do, give the Tri-Town Times a call. I'd be more than happy to write up a piece on you for the paper."

His smile widened and his face softened as if he'd just met the kindest person alive. "That's nice of you. What did you say your name was again?"

"Tilly. Tilly Bordeaux."

"I'll keep that in mind."

"Take care, Mr. Hill," I said over my shoulder as I walked away. Derek's good nature seemed to be rubbing off on me. Not that I'd been a mean and nasty woman before, but I'd lost a lot of faith in humanity when Tommy left. Doing nice things for others felt really good.

When I opened the car door, the papers flew around inside the cab. I glanced at the building and noted a small dumpster by the side of it. Might as well take care of my garbage problem now instead of waiting until I got back to Oak Peak.

I grabbed the papers and walked over to the

dumpster. When I lifted the lid, I noted two containers marked Rat Poison.

I stared at them a second and memorized the brand, then threw in the papers and shut the lid.

Interesting.

Jake had been poisoned, but I didn't know what the substance had been. Darryl Hill had two containers of poison, but he'd also thought he had a rat problem, so they could have been purchased to deal with that. It was something to keep in mind moving forward, especially if I could find out what type of poison the murderer had used.

I pushed opened the lid again, glanced around the empty parking lot, then pulled out my phone and quickly snapped a few pictures of the bottles. When I got those, I stepped back and took a few shots of the dumpster and finally, the front of the building with the dumpster visible in the frame.

Regardless of his claims of innocence, Darryl Hill had motive, and I might have discovered the weapon.

13

AFTER CLOCKING in a few hours at the office, I arrived home just before the sun set. My breath caught as I pulled into my driveway. Gone was the forest of death. I'd become so used to gazing at the burnt trees, to catch sight of the pristine, clear land, shocked me.

I slid out of the truck and walked toward the back fence. For the first time, I could see the old Rupert house... or I should say the new York home. It seemed far away but really, the distance was only about four acres.

Tinker trotted next to me, and I was so enthralled with my new view, I didn't watch where I put my feet. I lost my balance and fell to my hands and knees. Pain shot up my ankle and into my shin as I turned and sat down. I'd twisted my foot in a hole Tinker had dug in the grass. She stared at me with her tail wagging.

"You know better than to dig, Tinker," I said, rubbing the side of my calf. Nothing seriously hurt; just another accident that would require some ibuprofen and possibly an ice pack.

She lay down next to me and placed her head on her paws, her big brown mournful gaze trained on me. I had a feeling she wasn't apologetic that she'd dug the hole, but sorry that I'd gotten caught up in it.

"It's all right," I said with a sigh as I tapped her head. "I still love you. I hope you got whatever you were looking for."

I staggered to my feet and continued my trek to the back fence when I noticed Minnie dressed in leggings and a sweatshirt crossing her pasture toward me, Tulip and Sunflower at her heels. Her legs were so thin, I wasn't sure how they held up the rest of her body.

"The last person I want to see," I muttered as I smiled and waved. Tinker also saw them approaching and ran for the chicken coop. Apparently, she didn't like the cows, or their owner, either.

We met where the fences merged.

"Hi, Tilly!"

"Hey, Minnie."

Even though it was cold enough for a light jacket, Minnie's face was covered in a sheen of sweat. Obviously, she'd been exercising.

"I'd just finished my second workout for the day in the barn when I saw you," she said, dragging her sleeve across her forehead. "How are things going?"

"Good. Everything's great. How about you?"

"Excellent."

Tulip and Sunflower sandwiched Minnie and leaned their heads over the fence to get a sniff of me. I pet them, hoping they'd back off a bit once they'd gotten a noseful.

"What do you think of the Ruperts' place?" Minnie asked.

"It certainly looks different," I replied. "I do miss the orchard though. Not the burnt version, but the one with the flowering trees."

Minnie glanced over at the barren plot of land. "I know Tulip and Sunflower miss the nectarines, but I'm glad the trees are gone. They played havoc with my allergies when in bloom."

Tulip and Sunflower should never have been in the orchard, but often found their way there thanks to Mrs. Rupert loosening the fence and her hatred of the trees.

"Well, it was nice of Derek to take it upon himself to buy the property and clean it up," I said. Tulip nudged my hand again.

"Oh, yes. He's an excellent neighbor. So much better than his cranky father."

I absently pet the cows and tried to figure out a way to end the conversation. The only reason Minnie thought Mr. York had been cranky was because he didn't like Tulip and Sunflower in his yard eating his flowers. Minnie and her cows had no boundaries.

"I was wondering if you heard what happened today in Cedarville."

"No," I replied. "I was in Little River most of the day."

Minnie crossed her arms over her chest and shook her head, then grimaced in disgust. "There was another anti-Mexican protest outside of Martinez's Mexican Fiesta."

I stared at her a moment, unsure if I'd heard her right. "Another anti-Mexican protest?"

"Oh, yes. Same people as last time."

"Last time?"

"About six months ago. Don't you remember that?"

I scrounged my memory, trying to figure out

what exactly she was talking about. Were the protestors angry about the food or the people?

For the life of me, I couldn't recall any mention of an anti-Mexican protest at the restaurant. I would think Carla would have said something since that had been back when she actually spoke to me on a regular basis and didn't ignore my calls.

"What happened?" I asked. "I don't remember anything about any of this."

Minnie rolled her eyes and shifted her weight. "Tilly, you're supposed to be the reporter around here. How can you not know these things?"

I smiled and wished my good upbringing allowed me to be just as rude. "Enlighten me, Minnie."

She began with a loud sigh. "About six months ago, I was eating at Jake's Mexican Fiesta with a friend from out of town. The place was mildly crowded—about half-full. All of a sudden, we heard loud shouts coming from outside. There was a group of people in the parking lot holding signs and chanting, 'Go Home! Go Home! America is for Americans!' Garbage like that. I honestly couldn't believe it."

I couldn't either. It always shocked me when I

heard there were people alive today who acted in such a disgusting manner.

"Now, I'm not for open borders or anything like that, but—"

"How many protestors were there?" I really didn't care about her views on immigration.

"Oh, maybe five. But they were quite rowdy. The guy in charge was the loudest."

"Did you know him?"

"Oh sure," Minnie replied. "It's Tucker Browner."

I'd never heard of him. "Funny he's a racist with that last name."

"Don't I know it," Minnie replied with a snicker. "He's a farmer in Cedarville and as cranky as a summer day is long."

"What happened next?" I asked.

"Well, the owner, Jake, went outside and really got into Tucker's face. I thought fists were going to fly. The yelling, the language... it was a sight to see. Tucker kept screaming at Jake that he needed to go back to Mexico. Jake warned that if he didn't get off his property, he'd make him very sorry."

"What did he mean by that?"

"I don't know." Minnie stroked Sunflower. "He didn't specify."

"What was Tucker's response?"

"He said, and I quote, 'The only good Mexican is a dead one.'"

Bile rose in my throat as the ugly words sank in.

"So you were outside during the whole thing?"

"Oh, no. Jake had those little windows open to let the summer breeze blow through. It carried the conversation, if you could call it that, right into the restaurant."

"That's awful. Did anyone call the cops?"

Minnie shook her head. "No. The whole thing was over in minutes. Jake came back into the restaurant and apologized profusely to everyone. Someone said something about calling the police, and Jake asked them not to. He then turned up the fun mariachi music to drown out the idiots in the parking lot, closed the windows, and had margaritas and fried ice cream delivered to all the tables."

I let out a long breath I didn't realize I'd been holding. "It sounds like a horribly tense situation."

"Oh, it was. But Jake quickly muffled it all with alcohol and sugar. Of course, I didn't have any of that."

Of course. Minnie's desire to be fit and thin seemed to override any fun that may come into her life.

"And Tucker was back at it again today in front of the restaurant?"

"Yes! I can't believe you didn't hear about it."

"Like I said, I was in Little River most of the day. How did you know about it?"

"One of my friends had lunch there this afternoon and phoned to tell me about it."

"And did anyone call the police today?" I asked.

"My friend didn't say. She was leaving as they started their disgusting chants. But something needs to be done about Tucker. The man's a disgrace to our community."

I fully agreed, but people couldn't be policed for their beliefs, only their actions. And if Jake hadn't wanted to prosecute Tucker during the summer and no one had called the sheriff earlier, there was nothing that could be done. Maybe the police could have arrested him for disorderly conduct, but I couldn't think of much else, although there was probably something. I wasn't a cop. Perhaps trespassing? I didn't know the laws on such matters.

Minnie looked over at the Ruperts' land for a long moment, her head tilted to the side as if she were in deep thought. "Do you think Tucker Browner could have killed Jake?"

The only good Mexican is a dead one.

"I... I have no idea," I said, my heart thundering. The thought wasn't something I'd considered, but it definitely should be explored.

"Well, someone should tell the sheriff about it." Minnie ended her comment with a nod and narrowed gaze.

"You're right," I replied. "Someone should."

I had a feeling she was volunteering me.

"Let me know what he says," she said. "I should get back to the house. It's time to give my babies their vitamins."

Tulip nudged my hand again, then sneezed. Snot shot out her nostril and landed on my shirt and arm. She then turned and followed Sunflower and Minnie.

I hated those stupid cows.

With a sigh, I walked back to my own house. Minnie was right—the cops should know about Tucker's protests and what he'd said.

I also couldn't help but wonder if Jake wanted to take matters into his own hands with Mr. Browner, and that was why he hadn't wanted the police called. After what I'd learned about how he'd sent Darryl Hill out of business, I wouldn't put anything past him.

What if Jake had retaliated following the initial

protest, and the whole dispute escalated into Tucker killing Jake?

Or what if Tucker simply did believe the only good Mexican was a dead one and he'd followed through? Did that mean Sophia and José were in danger as well? Would he be coming for them next?

Darryl Hill, Sophia, José, Jerry the farmer... they were all on my radar as possible killers, but now it looked like I had another one to add to the list: a racist with an ugly heart.

14

———

THE NEXT MORNING, I popped into Debbie's to check in. The bakery was crowded with only one table available, so I hurried through the swarm of people and grabbed it. At the next table, I found Mrs. Markle, a woman in her seventies. Born and raised in Oak Peak, she was a town treasure and commanded respect wherever she went.

"Hi, Mrs. Markle," I said as our gazes met, her clear, blue eyes shining with kindness.

"Hello, Tilly. Lovely day, isn't it?"

The woman also seemed to know everyone. I'd had a couple of encounters with her, and she always called me by my name.

"It is," I replied. "Winter is around the corner, though. I can feel it in the air."

"Agreed. When you get to be my age, you feel it in your joints."

We chatted a few more minutes and she returned her attention to her coffee.

I waved at Debbie as she served her customers. Although she smiled and chatted briefly with everyone, she had deep bags under her eyes. She definitely needed some help, and I wished she wasn't such a control freak so she could actually hire someone and allow them to do their jobs without hovering over them.

Twenty minutes passed before everyone had their order. When the crowd thinned out, Debbie walked over and sat down across from me. She pushed a coffee with cream toward me.

"Good morning," I said.

"Is it really still only morning? I feel like it should be about six at night."

"Sorry. It's not even nine."

"Oh, my word. It's going to be a long day." She glanced around the store, then leaned in and lowered her voice. "I have some information for you."

"What's that?" I asked, bringing my voice down to almost a whisper.

"There's a farmer over in Cedarville. His name's Tucker Browner. Yesterday, he was over at Martinez's

Mexican Fiesta with a few other folks chanting things like go back to Mexico, and the only good Mexican is a—"

"Way ahead of you on this one, Debbie," I said. Leaning back in my chair, I took a sip of coffee, satisfaction rolling through me. "I heard about this yesterday."

Debbie stared at me for a long moment, her eyes wide. Finally, she blinked. "You knew this?"

"Yes. I beat you to it."

I couldn't help but giggle at the look of horror that came over her face.

"Good Grief. I'm slipping. Who told you?"

"My neighbor, Minnie."

Debbie rolled her eyes. "And how did she find out? Was she there?"

"No, but her friend was."

"So a direct source of knowledge—not word on the gossip vine. Okay, you win."

We both grinned and drank our coffee.

"What do you make of it?" she asked.

"I'm not sure," I said with a sigh. "Except it's ugly and I'm shocked that there are people in this world who can still look at another's skin color and have such hatred."

"Agreed."

"But this isn't the first time Tucker Browner has protested the restaurant."

"That's what I heard," Debbie said. "Last time, he and Jake Martinez almost came to blows."

"Excuse me," Mrs. Marple said from the next table. Both Debbie and I turned. "I'm sorry for eavesdropping, but there's something else you should know about that horrid man, Tucker Browner."

She smiled politely as the light shined through her gray bouffant giving her an angelic, halo-like appearance, yet, her eyes gleamed with the mischief of someone about to reveal a secret.

"What's that?" Debbie asked.

The older woman looked around the store as if to make sure no one heard what she had to say. Her family had been one of the original founders of Oak Peak, and when she spoke, people listened.

She pulled her chair over to our table and sat down with her coffee. "Tucker Browner used to also picket Darryl Hill's restaurant up in Little River until he found out Darryl was white."

"Really?" Debbie asked.

"Yes," she whispered. "My daughter, who works in a bar up in Little River said she overheard a conversation between the two about Jake Martinez."

"What did they say?" I asked.

"Well, Tucker Browner apologized for thinking he was Mexican because he owned the restaurant. A really vile man, if you ask me. But he bought Darryl more than a few drinks and, according to my daughter, they decided they were going to devise a plan to get rid of Jake Martinez for good."

Debbie and I exchanged looks, and I noted in her gaze she thought the same thing as me: we may have found our killer, or in this case, killers.

"Did they actually say they were going to murder him?" I asked.

"She didn't hear that, but the bar was terribly busy that night. They like to get their drink on up in Little River."

"But she heard them conspiring to do something?" Debbie asked. "She's just not sure what."

"That's correct," Mrs. Marple said. "They had imbibed far too much and staggered out of the bar together, both boasting they were going to take care of Jake Martinez once and for all. But what that meant, no one knows. Based on what my daughter told me, I'd be surprised if either even remembered having the conversation."

I let out a long breath I didn't realize I'd been holding.

"Someone should tell that no-good sheriff," Mrs. Marple said, then took a sip of her coffee. "Everyone realizes he wants to have this murder solved by election time so he can brag about what a great cop he is."

"When did your daughter hear that conversation?" I asked.

Mrs. Marple narrowed her gaze as she stared at the table. "Maybe a month or two back."

"So, long after Darryl's restaurant had been shut down."

"Oh, yes. Tucker began holding his silly protests out in front of Darryl's restaurant almost immediately after it opened. He put a stop to it once he realized Darryl was white."

"Did they come into the bar together that night your daughter witnessed?" Debbie asked.

"She didn't say. It could have been a chance meeting, or they could be thick as thieves."

"Well, that certainly adds a new dimension to finding out who killed Jake Martinez," Debbie said.

"Are you trying to find out who murdered him?" Mrs. Marple asked, her gaze firmly on me.

I didn't want to admit that I was looking into it, so I tried to deflect. "Why do you ask that?"

"Because you solved Henry York's murder."

Under Mrs. Marple's intense scrutiny, I felt like a child about to be caught in a lie.

"The police in this area aren't smart enough to find the killer, dear," Mrs. Marple said as she rested her bony hand over mine. "They're good for rounding up cows and changing tires for stranded motorists, but murder is above their pay grade."

Mrs. Marple slowly stood and gathered her purse from the back of her chair. "Sheriff Connor will want someone in custody before the election, even if it means that person isn't guilty of this crime."

"He's already focusing on my friend who worked for Mr. Martinez," I said. "But I don't think she did it."

She nodded and pursed her lips together. "Then it's up to you, Tilly Bordeaux, to find out who did. You can't allow your friend to go to jail."

"Thanks for letting me know about Tucker and Darryl's meeting," I said. I appreciated her vote of confidence, but I wasn't ready to admit I was actively trying to discover who had committed the murder.

"Of course. Be careful in your pursuits of the truth," Mrs. Marple said with a smile. "You're treading in dangerous waters, dear."

As she turned and walked out of the bakery, I sat down again. "That was interesting."

"Yes," Debbie replied with a yawn. "That woman doesn't like the sheriff one bit."

"You're right about that. She's not the only one. Harold is running a piece in the paper on him, as well as his opponent. It should be exciting to hear what people think, and I hope they want him gone and new blood in the office."

"I'm looking forward to reading about it," Debbie said. "I think the office needs someone new, but the person also has to fit into our community and have our values."

"The guy running is from out of town. I think I heard Chicago?"

"Well, I'm not sure he'll do well here with that background. We'll have to see what the voters say."

I sipped my coffee while Debbie's gaze jumped all over the restaurant like a mother hen keeping her eye on her chicks.

"How's your romance going?" Debbie asked, eyeing me over her cup as she brought it to her lips.

"It's good. Thanks for setting him straight on the sugar-free donuts."

"Of course. I really like him, Tilly. He's cute, polite, and totally digs you."

Heat crawled up my neck and into my cheeks. "Well, I like him, too."

"You should get married."

"No way," I replied, shaking my head. "Just the thought makes me want to vomit."

Debbie laughed and set down her cup. "Now you sound like me. I'm not one for that life."

"You're married to the bakery."

"That's true. And it's a relationship that works well for me. I don't have to compromise on what I watch on television, pick up dirty socks and towels, or listen to anyone's snoring."

We both giggled, and I wondered if Derek left his dirty clothes lying around the bedroom. I'd been over to his house a few times, and it had always been clean, but I'd never seen the upstairs.

"What's on your agenda for the rest of the day?" Debbie asked.

"I'm not sure," I said with a sigh. "I was thinking of going to see Sophia again and asking a few questions about Tucker, just to gauge her reaction, but I don't think I'll have time. I've got loads of things to do at the paper. And after what Mrs. Marple just told us, I think we have to add Tucker to the list of suspects, along with Darryl Hill."

"Agreed. Just be careful, Tilly. You can only hide behind the guise of writing articles for a little bit before people start questioning why you're so nosey."

"I know. But I'm not letting Carla go to prison for a crime she didn't commit. I have to find the killer."

15

I ARRIVED home that afternoon to Derek sitting on my porch swing with Tinker lying next to him, her head in his lap while he stroked her brow. She opened her eyes when I parked my truck but didn't move to greet me as she usually would.

"Traitor," I muttered. "I see you like Derek more than me now."

"Hey!" he said as I exited the cab.

"This is a nice surprise!" I exclaimed, climbing the steps. I had to admit, I was thrilled to have him waiting for me. "What are you doing here?"

"Well, I've spent most of my day missing you and wishing I could see you."

"You should have called and met me for lunch," I

said, gazing down at him. His eyes were blue in the twilight, and his smile warmed my soul.

"I thought about that," he said as he slid out from under Tinker and stood. "But I know that if you get all your work done, you tend to come home a little early." He placed his hands on my shoulders. "I wanted you all to myself for more than a lunch hour."

Standing on my tiptoes, I gave him a little kiss. "You're super sweet, Derek. I'm glad you're here."

"Me, too. How was your day?"

I pulled out my keys and unlocked the door. "It was fine." I motioned him inside. "Nothing exciting. What about you? What happened in the life of my millionaire neighbor today?"

Derek grinned. "I got some exciting news."

"What's that? Do you want some tea?" I set down my bag on the counter.

"I'm good. No tea for me. But I've been invited to speak at a halfway house in Los Angeles."

After pouring myself a glass, we both sat at the kitchen table. "A halfway house is where people go after rehab, right?"

"Exactly. They learn more skills to integrate back into society and work on their sobriety. Sometimes, after detox and rehab, it's daunting to head home, to get back to reality. It's a safe place for those in recovery to learn how to live their real lives without drugs or alcohol."

"And they asked you to speak to their members?"

Derek nodded. "I spent about six months at this particular one and they reached out to me to see how I was doing, which was weird because I haven't been there in ten years. When they heard that I'd kept my sobriety, they asked me to come speak to their guests. I guess I'm one of the rare ones who learned to function without drugs, and they want me to share my story."

I could hear the pride in his voice and my chest swelled for him. He was a good man who fiercely protected his sobriety, and I admired him and his dedication to his clean lifestyle.

"That's great, Derek," I said, sipping my tea. "When do they want you there?"

"I have to leave tomorrow."

Disappointment settled in my heart and I realized I'd miss him. "So soon?"

"Yes. I won't be gone more than three days, though. Two days to travel and then a day for my talk."

"Okay, good," I replied with a smile. "I think I can survive that."

"I'm really looking forward to it. I hope I can make a difference in at least one person's life."

I stared at him for a moment as I sipped my tea. If our relationship was going to move forward, I wanted to know about his past. He seemed to be a wonderful person today, but there'd been a time that wasn't the case. Tomorrow he would be stepping back into that life to offer advice to those aiming to take the same path as him. I had to understand who that man had been ten years ago.

"Tell me about when you were on drugs," I said. "I'd really like to hear about it."

His smile faded as he cast his stare down to his hands. "I did a lot of things I shouldn't have."

"Like what?"

He squirmed in his chair and I could see I'd made him terribly uncomfortable. I almost cut the conversation, but then he met my gaze.

"I stole not only from my parents, but from anyone I could. I broke into houses during the day when people were at work and took what cash I could find, as well as jewelry and anything else I thought I could sell. I robbed people on the street at knifepoint. Sometimes I lay in bed at night and see the faces of those I threatened. They'd been so frightened. Some had begged for their lives while I laughed. Those memories make me sick to my stomach."

"Did you ever hurt anyone?" I asked, feeling a little ill myself.

"No."

Derek's drug addiction had fueled a pretty hard-core lifestyle and made him into a criminal.

"My sobriety is something that's on the line every day," Derek continued. "It's easier now than it was ten years ago, but I need to choose each day not to seek out heroin. I take one day at a time."

Although I'd never try to compare my relationship to food with his relationship to drugs, there were some similarities. Both of us were required to be decisive every day on situations that most people wouldn't think twice about. Derek had to decide not to do drugs, and I had to choose not to eat myself into oblivion, especially on days when things weren't going my way, and even on days when I had big wins in life. I always had to remind myself that food wasn't a reward and find other ways to celebrate my successes.

"Did you ever go to prison for your crimes?" I asked.

He shook his head and sighed. "No. Surprisingly, I was never caught. Looking back, it probably would have been a blessing in disguise if I had been. At least then I would have been forced to get sober, even if it only lasted for a while. It was a horrible time in my life."

"Did you live on the streets?"

"After my parents kicked me out for the final time, I did. I moved to Los Angeles where drugs were easier to get, and that's when I started committing crimes. Drugs can be found around this area, but you have to know the right people in order to score."

Drugs could be sought out anywhere these days, even in the little Tri-Town area. This thought truly made me sad. The addiction had almost cost Derek his life.

"Moving to L.A. must have been scary," I said.

"It was. Sometimes it felt like each day was a fight for survival."

Silence blanketed us, except for Tinker's soft snores.

"Thank you for telling me all this," I said. "I can see it's not easy for you to talk about."

We both smiled and he reached across the table to hold my hand. "It's not. Mainly because I was afraid that if you knew what I had done back then, you wouldn't want anything to do with me now."

Byron's words came to mind: once a druggie, always a druggie.

But I didn't believe that. I had proof sitting across from me at my kitchen table that with determination, it simply wasn't the case.

"Well, I happen to trust the theory that people can change," I said. "You have a daily battle to fight, and I have full faith you'll continue to win, Derek."

"Thank you for saying that," he whispered. "It means a lot to me."

"Of course. I believe it. And besides, everyone needs someone in their corner, cheering them on with their battles."

He shot to his feet and began pacing my kitchen. "I feel like a huge boulder has been taken from my shoulders."

I laughed as I watched him. With each step, he seemed a little lighter on his feet. After a moment, he sat down again and took my hand in his. His touch sent a shiver over my skin. "Before the conversation got so heavy, I was going to invite you over for dinner... and to spend the night."

We hadn't shared more than a few kisses and some serious cuddles, and this new development gave me a case of nervous excitement. However, I felt ready to take our relationship to the next level, especially now he'd been so open and honest with me about his past.

"I'd like that."

The smile that spread over his face gave me the giggles. Jeez, one would think he'd just won a yacht cruise or something.

"I didn't think you'd say yes," Derek said softly as he squeezed my hand. "I know you want to take things slow."

"Well, I did say that," I replied. "And I appreciate you giving me time and space while I found myself again. My ex, Tommy... he just destroyed me emotionally and I lost all my self-esteem. It's taken a long time, but I feel good about myself now, and us. I really like you, Derek."

Two months ago, I never would have been able to get the words out, but now, they flowed freely.

"I like you, too, Tilly," he whispered, his gaze firmly on me. Our stares locked for a brief moment, then he pursed his lips. "And that's why I worry about you."

He knew I hadn't been sharing the whole truth

about what I'd been up to—I could see it in his eyes and feel it my heart. I'd told him I wouldn't investigate Jake Martinez's death, and I'd been terribly evasive when he'd asked about it.

My cheeks warmed with guilt and I stared down at the tabletop. It was my turn to feel shame for my actions.

"Please be careful," he said. "You're dealing with a murderer, Tilly. Whoever it is, they've already killed one person, and I don't want you to be next on the list."

I didn't try to deny or sugarcoat it. Instead, I nodded and met his gaze. "I will. I promise. Right now, everyone thinks I'm just collecting information for the paper."

"You're going to knock on the wrong door at some point, say the wrong thing. You won't even know you've done it. Then, they may come after you."

"I know," I said with a sigh. "I just wish that stupid sheriff would do his job."

"He thinks he is."

"Well, he's not," I said, getting to my feet to put my glass into the sink. "He's a sexist turd who is only worried about reelection, not putting the right person behind bars."

Derek came up behind me and circled his arms around my waist. "You know, that's one thing I love about you—your dedication to finding the truth. Just be careful while you do it, okay?"

As I leaned my head back onto his shoulder, I placed my hands on top of his. "I will. I promise."

I appreciated the fact that he didn't lecture me or try to stop me. Derek may not approve of me searching for the killer, but he knew how much I cared for Carla, even if she wouldn't return my phone calls. The sheriff had her in his crosshairs, and I wouldn't allow my friend to go to prison.

Derek gave me a quick kiss on the cheek, then let me go. "I'm going to head home and get dinner started. How does fresh, homemade pizza sound?"

"Amazing," I replied, and my stomach growled. "I'll be over right after I feed Tinker, Belle, and the chickens."

"Great! And if Tinker and Belle want to spend the night at my house, they're welcome. The chickens will have to stay here, though."

"Oh, trust me," I replied with a laugh. "They aren't invited."

I followed him to the front door and watched him walk across my property onto his. With a sigh, I turned and began my chores.

That man had wiggled his way into my heart and I really looked forward to the evening ahead.

Hopefully, I'd be able to put the murder out of my mind for a while and simply enjoy being with Derek.

16

———

THE NEXT DAY, I arrived at Sophia's house unannounced. Color me shocked when I found a bunch of guys moving furniture inside. I didn't recognize any of them and as I sat in my truck, I wondered if Sophia had gone on another shopping spree. Yet, most of the stuff didn't look new. Could she be moving someone in?

José?

He came out of the house and picked up a box, then headed back inside.

"Of course," I muttered. "They aren't wasting any time."

I slid out of my truck and headed for the door. Sophia waved as I entered behind another guy with a box.

"Hey!" she said as she stepped to the side to allow him to pass. "I didn't know you were coming here."

She beamed with happiness, her eyes sparkling and a little tinge of pink in her cheeks. I may have thought she was making a mistake with José, but the situation agreed with her.

"Looks like you're getting some company," I said.

José came up behind her, wrapped an arm around her shoulders, and pulled her close possessively, all while eyeing me warily.

"Hi, José," I said with a smile. "It's nice to see you again."

"Tilly, right?"

"That's me!"

"What's going on?"

"Well, I'm the reporter for the Tri-Town Times, and I'm doing stories on the restaurant and Jake's death. I had a couple of questions for Sophia, and now that I see you're here, perhaps you can chime in as well?"

"Sure, I guess so," he said with a shrug. "I really don't have much to say, though."

"We're done here," one of the guys who had been carrying a box said as he came out of the house. "We'll see you later, José. Bye, Sophia."

"Wait! Aren't you going to help me unpack?" José called.

"We said we'd help you move," his friend yelled as he backed away from the house. "Not unpack your dirty underwear!"

"Thanks for helping us out, Carlos!" Sophia shouted as their friends got into the truck and pulled away. "Come on in, Tilly."

I followed the two into the familiar living room. Boxes were once against stacked on the couch. She had moved her dad out, and José in, darn quick.

"What's up?" Sophia asked once we were all seated. I had taken the same spot as the last time I visited.

"Well, I was just wondering if you'd heard anything about your dad's murder from the police. Any suspects?"

Sophia and José exchanged glances, then shook their heads. "No. The sheriff hasn't mentioned anyone."

"Which is a good thing because I'd have a few choice words for whoever he thinks did this," José said. "And maybe a couple of fists, too."

Sophia slapped his leg. "Stop it. You're all bark and no bite."

From what I'd seen and heard, I wasn't sure about that but I let the matter slide.

"Who do you think killed your dad?" I asked.

Sophia's smiled faded as she met my stare. "I honestly don't know," she said, her voice quiet. "If I think about it too much, I get really angry and upset. I have to trust the sheriff will discover who did it."

She may think differently if she knew the sheriff was looking at the person keeping the restaurant together: Carla.

I wouldn't discuss it with Sophia because I didn't want Carla to lose her job over something she didn't do, and after what I'd found out Sophia, José, and Jake had been capable of, I couldn't let them turn their vengeful sights on my friend.

"That's a good idea," I said with a grin. "I do have a couple of other questions, though."

"What's that?" José asked, still eyeing me warily.

I startled when I heard the voice from the hall-way. "Everything okay in here?" I turned to find Sophia's uncle, Tony, coming from the bedrooms.

"Everything's fine, Tony," Sophia said. "This is Tilly. She helped us at the restaurant when we reopened. Remember?"

I stood and stuck out my hand. "It's nice to see you again."

"Likewise," he said as our palms met. "Thanks for your assistance the other day. We really appreciate it."

I noted the slight lisp in his voice. Frankly, I'd forgotten all about Uncle Tony and his prison stint, and I'd never looked up what he'd done. Perhaps murder?

With his bright smile and friendly gaze, he didn't look like a killer. I released his rough hand, the sign of a man who worked in manual labor, and recalled Carla saying he'd been working at a farm down south for a while.

"I'm really sorry to hear about your brother," I said. His smile faded for a second and his eyes clouded over, but he quickly recovered.

"Thank you. I appreciate you saying that."

He moved a couple of boxes off the couch and sat down at the far end.

"I work at the Tri-Town Times," I said. "Jake Martinez's death is a big deal in our little community, so I was just asking Sophia and José some questions."

"Ah, I see."

"Would you mind answering a few?" I asked.

"Of course not."

"Can you tell me a little bit about your brother?

What your life was like growing up with him? Were you two close?"

What did you do that sent you to prison?

"Well, Jake was five years older than me. We were close when we were young boys, but once he hit his teens, we drifted apart. He was into girls and I was still stuck on the Power Rangers."

I nodded and made some notes. "Sophia told me that her father, and I assume you, grew up in Los Angeles, then moved up here. Did you relocate with Jake, or are you a recent transplant?"

"I came to Cedarville about three years after Jake. As we moved into adulthood, we became close, and I wanted to be near my brother after our parents passed."

"Do you help out at the restaurant a lot?"

"No," Tony said, shaking his head. "My main job is the farm. I'm actually part-owner now."

The pride in his voice was evident and when I glanced at him, I saw it in his eyes and smile. He seemed so different from what I'd heard his brother had been like.

"That's wonderful!" I said, and meant it. Going from prison to becoming a business owner was a big step. "What do you grow?"

"Mainly apples, but we have some cherry trees as

well. If you get an apple at the grocery stores in the Tri-Town area, it most likely came from us."

With a grin, I took more notes and hoped all my questions about his personal life seemed appropriate. Perhaps if things went well enough, I could dive into his journey to prison.

"What does this have to do with Jake?" Tony asked. "We're talking about me and you said you wanted to know about him."

Busted.

"W-well... the family dynamic in running a business has always been interesting to me. I'm sorry I ran off course there. But now I'm thinking it would make an interesting article, maybe even a series on local family businesses and how they operate."

"That would be really cool," Sophia said. "Have people focus on us and the restaurant instead of my dad's death."

"Exactly," I replied with a nod, surprising myself with my quick thinking. Honestly, it wasn't a bad idea and it gave me the excuse to pry a little bit more.

"It does sound interesting," Tony said, standing. "But right now, I've got to run. Besides, I may be family, but I'm not involved in the business." He pointed at José and Sophia. "Those are the two you want to interview. They're holding the restaurant together now."

"And Carla," I blurted. My friend wouldn't even return my phone calls because she was so involved with the restaurant, while the true owner, Sophia, was busy making puppy-dog eyes at José.

"Yes, we couldn't keep things running without Carla," Sophia said, also getting to her feet. "She's amazing."

My cue to leave. My shiny new idea of highlighting businesses run and staffed solely by family bounced around in my brain like a squirrel on crack cocaine. It would make a great series of articles for the paper once the murder was solved and we went back to publishing stories about the knitting club and the high school fundraisers.

I followed Tony out the door and waved at Sophia and José over my shoulder. Although I smiled, I still thought they were guilty. I just didn't know how I'd go about proving it.

As I headed toward home, my phone rang. Even though it was illegal to talk while driving unless one used hands-free calling, I picked it up.

"Tilly, it's Carla," she whispered into the phone.

I immediately pulled over into a parking lot. "Why are you whispering?"

"Because I found something I don't think I should have, and I'm afraid someone's going to come in and find me."

"Where are you?" I asked.

"The restaurant. Sophia and José should be here any moment and I don't know what to do."

"I'm about three minutes away," I said, pulling out of the driveway. My heart thundered as I tried to remain within the speed limit. "I was just with José and Sophia. They live too far out and can't get there before me. What did you find?"

"I... just come. I can't believe this."

Carla hung up and I took some deep breaths. It's not like she could have found another body, right?

Thankfully, the Martinez's Mexican Fiesta parking lot stood empty except for Carla's car. I slammed my truck into park, grabbed my keys, and ran to the door. When I found it locked, I banged my fist against it, and Carla answered moments later.

"José should be here by now to prep for lunch," she said as she locked the door. "Are you sure he's not on his way?"

"He's moving in with Sophia. I just left her house and they seemed pretty cozy. I have a feeling José is going to be late."

She grabbed my hand and pulled me through

the empty restaurant to the booth where we'd found Jake. A stack of ledgers lay on the table. The seat cushion had been removed and lay flat on the floor.

I gasped when I saw what was inside. "Oh, my word, Carla! What the heck?"

When I turned to my friend, tears gleamed in her eyes. "It's the missing money," she said. "Remember how I told you I could never get a raise and Jake always said that we didn't make any money?"

"Yes," I said, staring at the piles of cash.

"These are the ledgers." She placed her hand on top of the stacks. "He had two sets of books. The real ones, these, and the counterfeit ones, which he paid his taxes on."

I bent over and peered into the base of the booth.

"I think anytime we were paid in cash, he grabbed it. In fact, he used to encourage people to pay in cash by offering a five percent discount. I never understood why, but now I do."

"How much is in there?" I asked.

"I haven't counted it. A lot."

Yes, that would be a good description of what I saw. A heck of a lot.

"So he skimmed the cash and put it in here? And kept secret books on it?"

Carla pursed her lips and nodded as I straightened and met her gaze. "That's what it looks like to me. Since he's been gone, we've actually been doing really well, Tilly, except for that week we were shut down. I didn't understand how until now."

"How did you find it?"

"I sat down at this table to do the books for last night, except I sat over here." She pointed at the opposing chair. "I put my feet up and I guess I pushed on the cushion, and it moved. At first I thought it would be another expense because it should be fixed even though we never seat anyone here, but then I saw the money."

I plopped down in a booth across the aisle. "What are you going to do?"

Carla picked up the ledgers, threw them on top of the cash, then slid the cushion back into place.

"I don't know, but I do wonder if Sophia and José know about this. My guess is that there's easily a couple hundred thousand dollars in there."

Our gazes locked, and I could see for the first time since Jake's death, we were both on the same wavelength.

"And that's a reason for murder," I said as we both nodded.

17

———

Ideas began coming to me like rockets through the night. Before I got a chance to express any of them, Sophia's voice wafted through from the restaurant's kitchen.

"They've arrived," Carla whispered. "Go out the front door. We'll talk about it later."

"They've already seen my truck in the parking lot," I said. "They know I'm here."

I glanced at what had become known as Jake's table. Receipts littered the top, and I figured they were in some particular order, knowing Carla. I grabbed her arm and pulled her a couple of seats down and motioned for her to sit. I slid into the booth across from her. "I didn't want to mess up your bookkeeping," I said. "We're just two friends talking."

"About stolen money."

"Shh!"

"Carla?" Sophia yelled. "Are you here?"

"Over on table ten!" Carla called.

Sophia rounded the corner and smiled, then tossed her wall of black hair over her shoulder. "I thought that was your truck out there, Tilly."

"Yeah, I haven't seen Carla in a while, so I decided to stop by since I was in the neighborhood." I glanced over at my friend who had paled and looked like she was about to be sick. "I'll be leaving in just a few minutes."

Sophia nodded and turned to my friend. "Did everything add up okay from last night?"

"Yes. The receipts matched the register down to the penny."

"Great! I'll go back and help José with the prep work. We're running a little late."

As she disappeared around the corner, I shot Carla a glare. "You have to pretend that everything is okay and you didn't find that money. You look like you're about to lose your breakfast."

"I feel like I am," she replied, placing her elbows on the table and her head in her hands. "I don't think I can act natural."

"Walk me outside," I said, standing.

The fall air blasted me in the face as I turned to her. "I suppose we should tell Sophia about the money. I mean, it's her restaurant."

Carla pursed her lips and crossed her arms over her chest. "I suppose you're right, but I'm angry, Tilly. I worked my butt off for that man and he told me he didn't make enough money to give me a raise. And the last time I saw him and we argued about it, he was literally sitting on stacks of cash. He died on top of that money."

"Jake was a jerk, and so is José. Sophia isn't nice, either. This place is like a hornet's nest. If you mess with it, they're going to attack. You need to get out of here, Carla. Find a new job. They're all crazy."

"What do you mean?"

I told her the abbreviated story version of the drowned rat in Darryl Hill's restaurant, and her mouth literally hung open.

"You're kidding me. I knew nothing about that."

"It's the truth. I've verified it with Mr. Hill and Sophia."

"She admitted to it?"

"Yes."

Carla shook her head and let out a long whistle.

"I'm going to leave," I said, taking her hand in

mine. "Please, get out of here. Start looking for a job today."

"I will," she replied, but I heard the hesitancy in her voice.

"Are you going to take some of the money?" I asked.

Her gaze met mine and I noted so much conflict in her expression. My friend sat square in the middle of a moral dilemma: should she steal the money, or leave it?

"I don't know. It would help Mac and me a lot. And it's due to me. Some of that is mine. I've busted my butt for too many years without being compensated for it."

Laying my hand on her arm, I nodded. "I get it, Carla. But if Sophia does know about it and finds some of it missing, you could be in a lot of trouble."

"I think she'd have taken it by now if Jake had told her about it."

"Maybe, maybe not," I said with a shrug. "It's in a safe place. You only discovered it by accident."

"True," she said with a sigh. "I don't know what I'm going to do."

"Keep me posted."

I walked to my truck and slid inside. Glancing at the clock, I couldn't believe it wasn't even noon yet.

A sigh escaped me as I put the gear into drive and headed out of the parking lot.

Of course, I wanted what was best for Carla, and to me that meant getting the money that was due to her. She'd mentioned time and time again how she'd helped the business by cutting costs, running the advertising efforts, and hiring the right people. For Jake to claim poverty as a reason for not giving Carla a raise was fine if it was true, but the fact that he'd been skimming money from his own establishment for years really upset me. I white-knuckled the steering wheel as I considered Carla's options. Would she be stealing if she took money that was rightfully hers?

Yes. It may be due to her, but it didn't belong to her.

Driving the thirty miles back to Oak Peak, my mind reeled. Martinez's Mexican Fiesta seemed to be the epicenter of immoral behavior, and the whole family was definitely bad news. The only one who seemed normal was Tony.

Which reminded me I had to look into why he'd gone to prison.

When I arrived back at the office, I was relieved to find it empty. After the morning I'd had, I really just needed some time to myself and to figure out what my next move would be to find Jake's killer.

I made a cup of coffee and sat down at my desk, the hum of the foot traffic and cars outside providing me with a lulling background noise as I fired up my computer and dived into the public records on Tony Martinez.

It didn't take long to find what I was searching for: he'd done a year in the state prison for extortion.

Interesting.

The case seemed pretty cut and dry. Tony had caught a farm owner, Brent Graves, having an affair and told him if he didn't pay up, he'd expose the relationship to the wife. Tony also hadn't been very smart and used his own phone to blackmail the man.

Mr. Graves hadn't liked that and he'd gone to the police and revealed the plan. Sheriff Connor had borrowed some equipment from state police and put a wire on the victim. When Tony showed up for the payoff, the police got what they needed and arrested him the next day.

Why not that night? Perhaps Sherriff Connor couldn't miss his baseball game or something just as absurd?

I called Sophia and asked for Tony's phone

number, telling her I just had a few more questions about his farm and his relationship with Jake. She gave it to me without any hesitation.

When Tony picked up, I heard a loud motor in the background.

"Hang on a second, Tilly," he said after I identified myself. "Let me turn off this equipment." A moment later, his end fell silent. "What's up?"

"Well, I looked up your prison record and I just have a couple of questions."

"Ah, man. C'mon, Tilly. I don't want to dredge that up and have it plastered all over the newspaper."

"I'm not," I replied. "It's just background information. I promise I just have a few questions."

"Fine," he said with a long sigh. "But please don't print anything about it. My family has been put through enough with Jake's death."

"I promise. It's old news that will remain buried. But I do wonder why the sheriff didn't arrest you that night? Why he waited until morning?"

A long pause ensued, and if I didn't hear the wind blowing, I would have sworn he'd hung up.

"I don't know why," Tony said. "But I can tell you, that wasn't me."

"W-what do you mean, it wasn't you?" I asked, furrowing my brow. "I'm confused."

"Jake ran that scam, not me. But he used my phone, which the cops traced back to me."

Jeez, my head was about to explode and I rubbed my forefinger between my eyebrows. "How... what?"

"I guess it doesn't matter now because Jake's dead. He knew the farmer. He saw him kissing someone who wasn't his wife. He contacted the farmer using my phone number, never thinking that Graves would turn him in. Jake went and got the money, but I don't know why they waited to make an arrest. That's something the police would have to answer."

Was Sheriff Connor really so incompetent, he couldn't tell the difference between the brothers' voices?

"Surely the sheriff realized he had the wrong man when he listened to you and the voice on the tape."

"No, he couldn't. Personally, I didn't think he wanted to be proved wrong, but Jake sounded just like me. Even threw in the lisp for good measure."

"What about your lawyer?" I asked, as I stood and began to pace the office. "Didn't he have the recording tested against your voice?"

"I didn't get a lawyer. Jake begged me to take the fall and plead guilty. He said that when I got out, he'd make it right, and he did. I own part of this farm now. Jake bought it for me."

"You went to prison for a crime your brother committed."

"Yes."

The depth of Jake Martinez's destruction of those around him truly astounded me.

"What happened to the money? Did Graves get it back?"

"Nope. The police searched my property for it, but I didn't have it. Jake took it and hid it somewhere."

Probably in the booth of his restaurant.

"Thanks for taking my call," I said, absolutely astounded and unable to bring up any other questions. "I appreciate your trust in telling me the truth."

"Sure, Tilly. Please don't print any of it. Sophia doesn't know and I don't want her to find out. She's been through enough."

"Of course," I whispered, then I disconnected the call and sat down behind my desk again.

Unbelievable.

"What in the heck is wrong with all of you?" I muttered as I stared at my phone. I'd never seen a family so dysfunctional. Jake had sent his brother to prison, and Tony seemed okay with it.

Or was he?

I pursed my lips together and tapped my pen on the desk.

Maybe Tony held a grudge. Had the whole experience infuriated him and he'd waited patiently until he could get his revenge?

Even though Jake had bought him a share in a farm, had it been enough repayment for spending a year in prison?

Or had Tony ensured that Jake would make the ultimate sacrifice for what he'd done?

"This list of people who may have murdered Jake gets longer every day," I said to the empty office, defeat weighing me down. "How am I supposed to figure out who is the killer?"

18

THE NEXT DAY, I hadn't heard from Derek, which didn't surprise me. He'd said he probably wouldn't be able to call until after he gave his talk, and I kept glancing at the clock wondering if he'd reach out at some point in the afternoon. I had to admit, I missed him more than I'd anticipated. Going home the previous night after discovering yet another layer of dysfunction in the Martinez clan, I had really wanted someone to talk with about it. Sure, I could have called Debbie, but I'd wished Derek had been there. Instead, I'd told Tinker and Belle about my day, and they'd listened almost as attentively as Derek would have.

My phone rang, and I answered after checking the caller ID.

"Hi, Sophia," I said, a little surprised at her call.

"Hey, Tilly. Tomorrow is my father's funeral. I was wondering if you could come and write something up about him for the paper. Overall, he was a decent guy who did a lot for the community."

I bit my tongue to hold back my true thoughts— Jake Martinez had been a self-serving psychopath— and almost said no.

However, I figured it may be interesting to watch the whole family together, as well as any friends who may attend. In the television shows, the murderer always went to the funeral. Perhaps it would be the case in real life as well.

"Sure, Sophia. Tell me when and where."

I wrote down the address and time, then hung up.

"Top of the morning, Tilly!" Harold said as he rushed through the door and set his computer bag on his desk. "How's my favorite reporter today?"

"Aren't I your only reporter?" I asked with a grin.

"You are, which by default makes you my favorite, especially if you completed the piece about the knitting club and their Booties for Babies program."

My chest clenched as I glanced around my messy

desk while trying to recall when he'd given me the assignment.

"I left you a note about it yesterday afternoon," Harold said. "Right there on your desk."

After moving a few papers, I shrugged. "Sorry, Harold. I don't see it."

He sighed as I pushed my chair back and found a sticky note on the floor. I picked it up and read the contact information for Lydia Tillwacker who headed up the Booties for Babies program.

"Found it!" I said, holding up the note above my head in triumph.

"You need to clean your desk," Harold grumbled. "A messy desk means a messy mind."

"I thought it meant abundant creativity," I said.

"Speaking of creativity, how's the book coming along?"

I'd started writing a mystery a few months ago, right after I'd solved Henry York's murder. It was proving much more difficult than I'd thought, but my goal was to see the finished product in the window of the town bookstore.

"I haven't worked on it in a while... in fact, ever since Jake Martinez died. But it's going okay. I'm having trouble coming up with murder plots, and I feel my characters are a little weak."

Harold threw his head back and laughed. "Sometimes truth is stranger than fiction. You've solved one murder, and you're neck-deep in reporting on another. Use your real-life experiences to add flavor to your manuscript, Tilly. I can't wait to read it."

I honestly hadn't given my book much thought the past couple of weeks. Between my infatuation with Derek, my worry over Carla, and learning about the dysfunction of Jake's family, I didn't have much brainpower to devote to creativity.

"Make sure you get that Booties for Babies article done for me by the end of the day," Harold said.

"I will," I replied. "In the future, perhaps it would be best if you sent me an email for things you need done."

"Yes, ma'am. Note taken. Emails will be sent in the future."

Harold could be a little rough around the edges at times, but overall, he was a good boss and I appreciated working for him. Such a far cry from Jake's relationship with Carla.

Once again, doubt crept into my mind.

What if she really had killed him?

I'd never seen her lose her temper to the point she came completely unhinged, but perhaps she had with Jake. I'd like to see the footage the cameras had recorded in the kitchen area of the restaurant for that night, but Byron had also said the cops were in possession of it. It's not like I could walk in and request to see it.

Or could I?

Not as Tilly Bordeaux, friend of the accused, but as Tilly Bordeaux, the reporter? I imagined that would require legal finagling that Harold simply couldn't afford. The paper wasn't really a job for him, but more of a hobby to stave off the boredom of retirement. He'd left the big career as an editor in Los Angeles. So I'd have to find out who did it without viewing the footage.

I stared at the post-it note in my hand and was about to make a call to Lydia Tillwacker, the head of the Tri-Town Knitting Club. Every year, they took on a different project. Last year it had been Handsies for the Homeless, where they'd knitted gloves and dropped them off at the homeless shelter in Cedarville. The paper had run a big article on it and included pictures of the ladies making their donations and a few homeless people wearing the gloves. The knitting circle had been so thrilled to see themselves in the paper, they'd purchased extra copies to send to relatives. Apparently, this year, they'd taken on the task of covering baby feet, and I imagined they'd make the donations to the hospital or maybe a women's shelter.

I picked up my phone and made the call to Mrs. Tillwacker. She was pleasant and very excited about her project. We spoke for about twenty minutes while I wrote down all the details of who was participating, when they were making the donation, how many booties they planned on giving away, etcetera. Then, I hung up and turned to my computer.

Halfway through the article, Doctor Wheeler walked in. My heart leapt into my throat as he waved. I recalled Harold telling me the doctor would let him know when the test results came back on Jake Martinez. I hoped we were about to find out the type of poison that killed him.

I stood and walked around my desk as he and Harold shook hands.

"Ms. Bordeaux," Doctor Wheeler said, taking my hand in his. "Lovely to see you."

"Thank you," I replied. "And thanks for stopping by."

"Well, I told Harold that I would let you know about the toxin that killed Mr. Martinez since he mentioned your office had a contentious relationship with the sheriff."

"That's a nice way to put it," I said with a grin. In

reality, I was the one who had burned that bridge. Harold had been an innocent victim.

"Well, I've submitted my report to the sheriff. Jake Martinez died of cyanide poisoning."

I stepped back as if he'd punched me in the gut. He'd made it clear he thought Jake had been poisoned when he'd arrived at the restaurant after Carla and I had found the body, but to actually hear it shocked me.

"The nachos had been laced," Doctor Wheeler continued. "The sheriff is concentrating on finding the source."

I raced back to my desk and grabbed my phone. I scrolled through the pictures of Tinker and Belle I'd taken the previous night—because they'd been so darn cute laying on the couch together—until I found the one I searched for.

When I'd gone to visit Darryl Hill, there had been rat poison in the dumpster. I used my fingers to enlarge the photo. Cyanide.

Darryl Hill had motive and he had the correct poison.

Doctor Wheeler and Harold made plans for lunch later in the week, then he left.

Harold turned to me. "That should narrow down

the suspects. Not everyone has cyanide lying around."

I nodded and sat down. "I just hope the sheriff does a thorough investigation. Last time we had the pleasure of speaking to him, he was pretty focused on Carla, but there are other people who benefitted from Jake's death."

Harold crossed his arms over his chest and furrowed his brow. "You've really been looking into this, haven't you?"

"Yes. I won't let my friend go to prison for something she didn't do."

"But Tilly, how do you know?" Harold asked softly. "Pull your emotions out of it for a moment and look at the evidence. First, she fought with Jake the night he was killed. She had motive. She had the opportunity. She was the last one to see him alive."

"I know all that," I replied with a sigh, "but I can't believe my friend would murder him. She had every reason to be upset with Jake, but I don't think she's got the heart of a killer."

Harold sat at his desk and propped his feet on top of a stack of papers. "Okay, let's talk this out. Go to the whiteboard and let's try to put your mind at ease."

"We don't have to do this," I said. "I know you're

really busy, and I have to finish my article on the knitting club."

"No, let's do this. You don't have faith in our sheriff and I can tell you're troubled by the thought of your friend being a suspect. Tell me what you've uncovered."

"Okay." I stood and went over to the whiteboard and picked up a pen. In the middle I wrote Jake Martinez and put a circle around the name. "Victim."

"Correct."

I then drew an arrow out to the left and wrote Sophia. "This is the daughter who is dating the chef at the restaurant named José."

He also received an arrow and I jotted his name down.

"How is a daughter and her boyfriend guilty of murdering her father?"

"Because they were dating and Jake didn't like it one bit. José got into a fight with him and told him he'd kill him if he tried to keep them apart. The three of them also worked together to terrorize the guy in Little River who opened a Mexican restaurant, Darryl Hill, by drowning a rat in his establishment and letting a few more loose inside. Then they called the Health Department and had him shut down."

I scrawled Darryl's name and an arrow pointing to it. "And Darryl just happens to have empty rat killer containers that contain cyanide in his dumpster outside his now-defunct restaurant. He was friendly with Tucker Browner, who is simply a piece of racist crap. They were going to, and I quote, 'take care of Jake Martinez once and for all.'"

Glancing over my shoulder, I noted Harold had paled.

"But it goes on," I muttered as I drew another arrow. "Jake's brother, Tony, went to prison for a crime he didn't commit. He took the fall for Jake, who in turn bought him a piece of a farm."

"Wow," Harold said, shaking his head. "What a mess."

"But it gets better. Or worse, depending on how you look at it."

"Seriously?"

"Oh, yeah," I replied as I made another line that had to squiggle through two of the other names. "A farmer Jake owed money to may or may not have threatened his life. It depends on how you took his statement."

"What did he say?"

"He said he thought things would be better once Jake was dead, but no one can figure out if he meant that he killed Jake and he thought he'd get paid, or if he thought things would be better after he heard of Jake's death. There's a big difference."

"I would agree with that. Did you hear him say that?"

"Yes. And I still don't know how to translate his statement."

Harold rubbed his temples. "I had no idea it would be this complicated. You have six people up there who wanted Mr. Martinez dead."

"He wasn't a very nice man, Harold. In fact, I would say he's probably burning in Hell right now. He hurt a lot of people."

The front door swung open and Debbie sauntered in, grinning ear-to-ear, carrying a plate of four donuts and three coffees. "I hired someone and I'm here to celebrate!"

Harold and I exchanged glances, then looked over at the woman. Her smile faded when she realized she'd walked in on something she shouldn't have.

"What's this?" she asked, her gaze shifting to the whiteboard. "Is this everyone?"

"Yes," I replied. "This is everyone we've suspected so far."

Debbie set the coffee and donuts down and

shook her head. For a moment, the three of us stared at the lines and names leading to where I'd written Jake Martinez. "What a darn mess," she muttered.

"I had no idea," Harold murmured.

"Do you see why the sheriff needs to investigate these other people besides Carla?" I asked. "There are a lot of suspects!"

"There certainly are," he said. "And you're right. These people need to be scrutinized closely. They all have motive and some have even made outright threats. I'm sure the sheriff will do his due diligence."

I snorted and rolled my eyes. "All he cares about is getting someone behind bars before the election."

"The truth will prevail," Harold said. "It always does."

I stared at the whiteboard, a feeling of dread settling over me. How did I untangle this web of lies and find the truth?

19

THAT EVENING, I scrolled through Facebook and found the halfway house where Derek spoke. They had posted pictures of him giving his talk, as well as photos of him afterward interacting with members one-on-one. His smile radiated, and I saw true happiness shining in his eyes. He thrived when helping others, and it only endeared him to me more. Dang it. I couldn't wait to see him. It seemed like he'd been gone weeks instead of a couple of days.

I sent him a quick text and asked him to call when he could.

The candy I'd picked up for the Oak Peak Halloween dance sat on my counter, calling to me, begging me to open the bag and eat a few pieces. I knew that one piece would lead to many more, and I didn't want that. Instead, I rose from the couch and hid them under the sink. Out of sight, out of mind. Derek and I hadn't discussed going to the dance being held at the community center, but I hoped we would attend. I'd been each year, and it was always a fun time, especially when Mac snuck in his hard cider. Last year, Debbie and I had gone as Burt and Ernie and giggled for hours after imbibing in a few cups.

My phone vibrated and I picked it up to see a text from Derek. Call you in a bit.

The wind howled outside and I turned on the television to drown it out. I hated the wind, especially living in such a remote area. It made me think of slasher movies and I imagined bad men with machetes sneaking around my porch, waiting for the perfect time to come through the window and chop me to bits.

I grabbed my laptop and decided to do a little research on cyanide. Jake Martinez hadn't died quietly. In fact, it appeared to have been a pretty painful experience. When we'd found him, his eyes had been open and his lips blue, covered in white froth.

According to the CDC, cyanide came in a gas

form, as well as crystal. Inhaled or ingested, it could kill you easily. It also could be found in plastic, and that's why no one should ever burn anything made from that material. Symptoms go hand-in-hand with the flu: dizziness, headache, nausea. These were only a few indicators of cyanide poisoning, and I recalled Carla telling me Jake thought he had the flu that night when he arrived at the restaurant. Either he had been sick, or he'd been exposed before he came.

Large amounts of exposure to cyanide caused convulsions, loss of consciousness, low blood pressure, and eventual respiratory failure.

No, Jake Martinez hadn't gone quietly into the night. He'd suffered quite a bit, and frankly, I found it difficult to scrounge up any pity for him.

My phone buzzed beside me and I grinned when I realized it was Derek.

"Hey!" I answered. "How are you?"

"I'm tired, but good. How are things there?"

I leaned back against the couch cushions and stared at the ceiling. "I'm reading about cyanide."

"Why?"

"That's what killed Jake."

"Wow," Derek said with a whistle. "What have you learned?"

"In big doses, it causes convulsions and respiratory failure."

"Didn't you mention he had white foam around his mouth?"

"Yes," I replied, sitting up. "Why?"

"Well, people get convulsions from drug overdoses, and those cause the foaming at the mouth."

"The doctor said that when we found him," I replied. "That it may be poisoning or a drug overdose."

"Honestly, they're very similar. Both can kill you. And let's face it—drugs are a form of poison."

I narrowed my gaze as I pet Tinker, who had jumped up on the cushion next to me. "Why do I get the feeling you're speaking from experience? Have you ever overdosed?"

"Yep. Not a fun time. I've seen it and I've been the one to do it."

"Oh, Derek," I said with a sigh. "I'm so glad you survived such a horrible time in your life."

"Me, too."

"When are you coming home?" I asked, suddenly having the need to grab him and never let go.

"I'll be leaving here in the early morning, so I'll be there in the afternoon."

"Jake's funeral is tomorrow. If you're back in time, do you want to go with me?"

"That sounds like one hot date," Derek said with a chuckle. "But yes, I'll be happy to go with the smartest, prettiest, funniest woman in Oak Peak. What time?"

My heart beat double time at his words, and I couldn't stop grinning even if I wanted. "Aww, you're so sweet. We have to be there at three."

"There shouldn't be any trouble with me being home by then unless there's bad traffic."

"Great!" I said, truly enthused. "I do have one more question."

"What's that?"

"Every year, Oak Peak has a Halloween dance at the community center. It's a lot of fun and I was wondering if you wanted to go together."

"Do we dress up?"

"Yes. Tickets are usually fifteen dollars, but you get a discount if you dress up, and then another discount if you bring five cans of food for the homeless shelter in Cedarville. We'll pay seven dollars each."

Not that it mattered to Derek, but it did to me. Fifteen wasn't a lot of money, but I tended to be frugal as I had to watch where every dollar went.

"Now that sounds like the kind of date I would love to go on," Derek said. "Will Debbie, Carla, and Mac be joining us?"

"As far as I know. We haven't really talked about it, but we've all gone together in years past."

"What should we go as?"

"I have some ideas," I said. "We can talk about them when you get home."

"Perfect. I'm heading to bed so I can get on the road early." He paused for a moment, and I wondered if he'd hung up. "I can't wait to see you, Tilly."

I grinned at Tinker and pursed my lips together. His words sent goosebumps over my skin. "Me too. Drive safe."

"I will. Bye."

Peace settled over me as I stared at my phone, yet, the longing for him sat heavily in my chest. I missed him so.

"Derek's coming home tomorrow," I announced to Tinker and Belle. "Isn't that fantastic news?"

Tinker's tail flopped on the cushion while Belle studied me with hooded lids from under the coffee table. "I can tell you two are excited as well."

I went back to my investigation of cyanide on the CDC website. The stuff was prevalent throughout humans' daily lives. In common food such as almonds, apples, and lima beans. Of course, it was also found in cigarette smoke, which didn't surprise me. However, discovering it occurred naturally in food certainly did.

"The stuff is everywhere, Tinker," I said. "In the soil and in common things we use every day. Did you know it's used to make paper and develop photographs? I had no idea."

Darkness had descended outside, and although I was tired, it was far too early for me to go to bed. I felt a little antsy and decided to make some of the banana bread Derek liked so much.

An hour later, the smell of the baking bread wafted through the house. Tinker now lay on the floor while I did the dishes. Belle had perched herself on the corner of the counter. I didn't like her up there, but frankly, I was tired of fighting her. If I chased her off, she'd only return. We'd been in a standoff over the counter since I'd adopted her.

"You win that fight, Belly-Belle," I said with a yawn. "Your persistence has paid off. I give up."

She meowed and stretched out across the tile, as if claiming victory on her space.

Once the bread was out of the oven and cooling

on the counter, I shut Tinker's dog door, turned off the lights, and made sure the locks were all set.

"Come on, my furry friends," I said, heading up the stairs. "It's time for bed."

Just as I settled into my pillows with Tinker on my left and Belle in between my legs, my phone rang.

I reached over a grabbed it off the nightstand, careful not to disturb my bedmates, then leaned back against my pillows.

"Hey, Carla," I said with a yawn. Perhaps I should have gone to bed earlier.

"Tilly, it's not Carla. It's Mac."

"Mac!" I said, quickly sitting up. Dread washed through me. Mac never called. "What a surprise! What's going on?"

"They arrested Carla tonight."

"Oh, no," I whispered as I cradled my forehead between my thumb and forefinger. "How? What happened? Tell me everything."

"She'd just gotten home from the restaurant. The sheriff rolled up with two deputies and they barged into the house with a warrant. We had to wait outside."

"Oh, Mac. I'm so sorry. That's what they did to

me. It's a sickening feeling, isn't it? How long were they there?"

"About a half-hour. We waited just outside the front door. It was so darn windy. I don't think we've ever been so cold. Then, they came out, and Sheriff Connor had a smug smile on his face. He arrested Carla and said we had cyanide in our garage."

"Did you?"

"We had a mouse problem a few years back," Mac said with a sigh. "I'd actually forgotten all about it. It was tucked away behind some other stuff on a shelf. The sheriff said Carla had motive, opportunity, and now he's found the weapon. She could go away for a long time if she's found guilty."

My worst nightmare had come true. That stupid sheriff had been so predictable. Now he'd be able to brag that he'd solved the murder and he'd be the hero in town. With that status, he'd get reelected. "Did you call a lawyer?"

"I did. He's meeting me down at the station in a bit, but I wanted to let you know what happened before I left the house."

"Okay, Mac. Keep me posted."

"There's one other thing, Tilly," he said, his voice lowering to almost a whisper. "Carla came home today with a bunch of money. When the police arrived, we'd just finished stuffing it in between the insulation in the attic. She said I shouldn't tell anyone about it, but she wouldn't give me any details. She said it was rightly due to her."

I pursed my lips together and closed my eyes, not sure if I should laugh or cry. "Yeah, don't say anything, Mac. It could only get her in more trouble."

We said our goodbyes, and after setting my phone down on the nightstand, I stared at the ceiling. The wind continued to whip and swirl around outside, the ominous feeling growing and morphing all around me.

Carla had stolen from the restaurant. I didn't blame her, but it wasn't right. However, that didn't mean she should be in jail for murder.

Tears welled in my eyes as helplessness spread through me. Who had killed Jake Martinez? I didn't think it was Carla. At least, I hoped not. More doubt crept into my mind with the knowledge she had the poison that killed Jake Martinez at her house, but I tried to push it aside. I knew my friend. She had a good heart. She may be able to steal money, but she didn't have the fortitude to kill someone.

It had to be someone in Jake's family, or any of

the other people he'd screwed over. He'd been a horrible human being and he'd ruined a lot of lives.

Tinker whimpered and snuggled in closer to me, resting her head on my stomach. She didn't like the wind, either.

As I stroked her brow and listened to the gusts rattling the house, sudden anger swelled within me and I clenched my fists.

Carla was innocent, and somehow, someway, I would figure out how to prove it.

20

I WOULDN'T HAVE time to come home before the funeral in the afternoon, so I wore black pants with a black sweater. The wind had also brought a couple inches of snow, so I also pulled on some black boots.

In the rural part of Oak Peak, our streets were always the last to be plowed. I left a bit early so I could take it slow. The icy air nipped at my cheeks, and I was thankful I'd also brought along my parka. I hoped the afternoon would offer some sunshine or the funeral was going to be an even more miserable experience.

As my day passed in the office, the ball of dread in my chest seemed to grow. I not only worried about Carla, but about Derek driving in the bad weather. I kept glancing out the window behind me, hoping I'd see his SUV. Would he make it back in time to join me at the funeral? With any luck, the highways down south hadn't been hit too hard and the plows could get through if necessary.

Around two-thirty, I accepted that I would be going alone. With a heavy heart, I looked over my shoulder once again and found Derek pulling up to the curb. I squealed in delight as I ran around my desk, crashing my hip into an edge. The contact took my breath away and I limped outside with tears stinging my eyes.

"Hey!" Derek said as he exited the car. His grin warming my soul, he walked over but quickly sobered when he saw me hobbling. "What happened?"

I wrapped my arms around his waist and reveled in his embrace. "Hit my hip on the desk."

"Are you okay?"

"Yes," I said with a sigh, then I tilted my head up for a quick kiss. "I'm great now that you're home."

"I just made it," he said. "Traffic was horrible. Are you ready to go?"

"Let me grab my coat and bag."

Derek waited outside while I hurried back into the office, collected my stuff, and whispered goodbye to Harold, who was on the phone. He waved and motioned me to call him later.

We held hands as we drove to the cemetery and for a few brief moments, it felt as if all was right in the world. Yet, I couldn't enjoy it. The wind and my worries had kept me awake a good portion of the night, so I was exhausted.

"Anything new since I talked to you last?" Derek asked. "I can tell you're preoccupied with something."

"They arrested Carla last night," I replied.

He squeezed my hand. "I'm sorry, Tilly. How did you find out?" His voice dripped with concern.

"Mac called me. They did a search of their house and found some cyanide, so the sheriff says that Carla has motive and now he's got the weapon."

"So things are looking bad for her."

"Yes, they are."

"We'll get it figured out, Tilly."

I turned to him and studied his profile as he drove. "I'm going to watch everyone at this funeral today. I think whoever could have done it will be there except Darryl Hill and Tucker Browner."

"The restaurant owner the Martinez's put out of business and that racist guy, right?"

"Yes."

"I agree. I can't imagine they'd show up to pay their respects."

The cemetery lay just outside of town on the way to Cedarville, and when we pulled up into the dirt parking area, Sophia and José were already standing by the casket.

We stared at them a moment, then Derek turned off the truck. "Well, let's do this."

"Do we have to?"

He glanced over at me and smiled. "You invited me, remember?"

"Yes, I did, and thanks for coming. I hate funerals."

"I don't think there's anyone who likes them."

As I stared at Jake's casket, I was taken back to the time my own father died when we lived in Kansas. He'd been working on a tractor out in the pasture and had a heart attack. We hadn't realized he'd been missing as he always spent hours out in the fields. When we found him, there hadn't been any hope of saving him.

We'd also had a funeral, and at ten years old, it had been a horrible and scary event for me. I remembered standing by my mother, holding her hand while they lowered the casket into the ground. She stood stoically throughout the funeral and the reception afterward held at our house, and I had tried so hard to mimic her, but failed. I ended up locking myself in my closet and bawling for hours. It wasn't until late that night that I saw my mother's grief. I heard her crying in the kitchen and snuck down the stairs. She sat at the kitchen table smoking a cigarette and drinking wine, surrounded by casseroles.

When our gazes met, she motioned me over as she stubbed out her cigarette. I crawled on her lap and we stared at all the food for a long while.

"What are we going to do with these stupid casseroles?" she whispered into my hair. "I don't want to eat any of them. Do you?"

I shook my head.

"We'll donate them to the church for the Sunday potluck. From this day forward, you and I are going to start over, Tilly. We're going to make a new life for ourselves, and it's going to be better. We aren't going to be eating the food that reminds us of your daddy's death."

Mama then sold the land we owned and moved us to Louisiana where she met my stepfather, Hank. He was so different from my dad. While my dad had been wiry, serious, and always worried about something, Hank was a larger man who loved to laugh and tell jokes. My father never had time for me—there was always something that needed to be done on the farm, something far more important than me telling him about my caterpillar that had turned into a butterfly or my day at school.

On the other hand, Hank always smiled, could find humor in just about anything, and he was always interested in hearing about my day. I loved him dearly, and sometimes the joy he emanated was what I imagined living with Santa Claus would be like. The difference between the two men was like night and day.

Mama had been right—our lives had changed, and definitely for the better. Both of us became happier being with Hank, which also brought along years of guilt for me. How could I appreciate someone more than my father? Sometimes, it still bothered me.

I hoped in a year or two, Sophia could say her life had become more positive with her father's death. She was young and there was still time to change her wicked ways. I found it difficult to believe that she could destroy someone's livelihood without a second thought, but she didn't have a good role model, either. Perhaps she'd turn her life around and find a path that didn't include intention-ally hurting others.

Derek and I walked hand-in-hand to the gravesite. The snow had melted, but left the grass mushy, and I was glad I'd worn my boots.

"Hey, Sophia," I said when we were a few feet away.

"Tilly. Thanks for coming."

"Of course."

José and Derek shook hands and for a moment, the four of us stood around awkwardly. It was hard making small talk with two potential murderers.

"I feel weird having you here since your friend has been convicted of killing my dad," Sophia finally said. "I hope you can keep your feelings out of it and write a decent article about him."

The hairs on the back of my neck bristled, but I tried to remain polite and turned my lips into a small smile. "Well, first, Carla hasn't been convicted of murdering your father. She's a suspect. Second, I'm perfectly capable of remaining impartial in any situation."

"Did you know the sheriff was looking at her?" Sophia asked, narrowing her gaze. "Were you covering for her?"

"No," I lied, my voice strong. "I had no idea."

Derek squeezed my hand, letting me know I was about to cross an unseen line.

"If she didn't kill him, then who did?" Sophia asked, her glare firmly in place. "You're just saying that because she's your friend."

"No, I'm not. I say that because there are too many other people who either wanted your father dead or threatened his life."

"Like who?"

"Let's sit down," Derek said, pulling me toward the chairs lined up around the grave.

He led me to two seats in the back row and my fury grew with each step.

Once seated, I turned to him. "How dare she—"

"Shh," Derek whispered. "We're here to observe, not to fight with her. You can do that later."

Clamping my bottom lip between my teeth, I vowed to remain silent. Derek was right. I didn't want to be kicked out of the funeral before it even began.

A few people I didn't know arrived, and I assumed they were family from out of town. Tony hurried up from the driveway carrying two brown grocery bags. He smiled and hugged Sophia and a couple of other people, then handed one of the bags to José, and another to someone else I didn't know.

The priest cleared his throat and everyone took a seat and quieted down.

As the service began, I found it hard to concentrate and counted about forty people in attendance. I studied them all and wondered who had killed Jake. José? Sophia? Tony? Had it been a family affair?

A shiver tore down my spine in the cold weather and Derek slipped his hand in mine. Somehow, some way, I had to find the killer and prove Carla's innocence.

In the distance, I noticed two men leaning against a tree, both of them staring at our group. One of them seemed familiar to me, and I squinted to try to make out his features. I gasped when I recognized Darryl Hill.

Why had he come to Jake's funeral? It certainly hadn't been to pay any last respects. And who was the other man? My guess was Tucker Browner, but I didn't know for sure as I'd never met the man.

They turned to each other and high-fived, then walked out of view down the hill.

Had that been a sign they were pleased with the murder they'd pulled off?

Why attend the funeral of a man who had ruined one of them?

I glanced over at Sophia. Her eyes remained dry,

but her brow had furrowed and she pursed her lips together as if she fought the tears. Our gazes met for a brief moment, and I saw the sadness there, but then she grabbed José's hand. She had everything she wanted now: no one to step in her way of being with the man she loved, the restaurant to make her own, and a home. If she played her cards right, she'd have a pretty good life.

When the service ended, Sophia came over to us. "We're having a little get together at the house if you two would like to come."

I glanced up at Derek, who nodded. "We'll be there," I said. "Thank you for the invitation."

Honestly, I didn't want to go, but I couldn't help but feel as though I were missing something. One of these people was a murderer; I felt it in my bones. There had to be a clue as to who that was. I just didn't see it yet.

I hoped, in the time I spent with them, the evidence would reveal itself.

21

I ESTIMATED about twenty people at the after-funeral reception. Derek and I sat on the couch and made small talk with those around us, which we found consisted of distant family from Los Angeles, as I had suspected.

"You're right," Derek whispered when we were finally left alone. "Those are some expensive appliances. I looked at replacing some in my house and I couldn't believe the prices on that stuff."

"I know. There's a ton of money sitting in there."

The bag Tony had handed to José sat on the kitchen table next to the assorted pastries and cakes wrapped up in Debbie's Deliciousness boxes. My stomach howled and I stood then meandered over, wondering if Sophia had purchased any of the sugar-free line.

As I tipped the lids and read the stickers, I noted the bag contained a bunch of apples. I didn't find any sugar free goodies and as I returned to my chair, my heart suddenly froze and I became paralyzed in place.

Apples.

Apple seeds contain cyanide.

I slowly turned and found Tony against the far wall. Our gazes locked. It all fell into place. Owning an apple orchard, he had access to as many apple seeds as he wanted. All he would have to do was dry them out, pulverize them, and he'd have ingestible cyanide that would be so small, it may look like some type of seasoning.

His gaze shifted away, then back at me. I turned to look at the bag of apples again, then at him. Tony's eyes flashed with fear, then settled into resolve.

He had the motive. His brother had sent him to prison.

He had the means—access to the restaurant and Jake's home.

He had the weapon. A damn orchard of them.

"You did it," I whispered.

Tony continued to glare at me.

I raised my hand and pointed at him while my heart thundered. I knew in my bones I was correct. "You did it," I said loudly. "You killed your brother."

Silence quickly fell and a few people gasped in surprise, their stares bouncing between me and Tony like they were observing a tennis match.

"You killed Jake," I said, slowly approaching him. You poisoned him."

Tony glanced around the house and shook his head. "No, I didn't. You're mistaken."

Yet, I could see it in his eyes.

"Jake died of cyanide poisoning," I said. "Apple seeds contain the poison, and you're part owner of a farm that has a whole orchard of them. You hated that your brother sent you to prison for a crime he committed. Killing him was your revenge."

"Tilly, what are you talking about?" Sophia said from the kitchen. "They arrested Carla. She did it."

"No, she didn't. Tony did."

"What do you mean they arrested Carla?" Tony asked, his eyes wide as he pushed off the wall.

"The sheriff arrested her last night," I said. "You killed Jake because you went to prison for him, and now, you've caused the same situation. Carla didn't kill your brother, and she's going to take the fall for it."

The heavy silence blanketed us. Tony's features went from shock to sadness in a heartbeat.

"Are you going to let an innocent woman go to prison for a crime you committed?" I asked softly.

"Uncle Tony!" Sophia wailed. "What's she talking about?"

Tony stared at me a beat, then his shoulders sagged as he moved his gaze to the floor. A man defeated.

"You're right," Tony said. "I did kill Jake."

Derek came up beside me and wrapped his arm around my shoulder. I'd been holding my breath and felt like my knees would buckle. I'd done it. I'd found the killer. Carla would be free.

"Why?" Sophia asked as she moved into the living room. "Why would you do that?"

Tony glanced around at his family and straightened his shoulders. "Because he was a horrible human being. I went to prison for a crime he committed. He didn't even think about admitting the extortion. He set me up. It was premeditated."

"I can't believe you killed my dad!" Sophia yelled, her hands fisted at her sides.

"Oh, come on, Sophia," Tony said, rolling his eyes. "Your father was horrible to you. Don't try to pretend otherwise. Don't be the victim."

"That doesn't mean I didn't love him!" she screamed as tears tracked down her cheeks.

"If he loved you, he would have treated you better and you wouldn't have ended up with a loser like José!"

I turned to face the kitchen. José stood by the counter, his gaze narrowed in fury.

"He's not a loser!" Sophia yelled. "I love him!"

"Even though he's been to prison?" Tony said, shaking his head. "Did he happen to mention to you that he's been to prison for aggravated assault with a deadly weapon?"

José came around the corner with flared nostrils and gritted teeth. "How did you know?"

Sophia stood in between them, glancing from one to the other while the two men stared each other down.

"I went to prison, José. Inmates talk because there's nothing else to do. I found out all about you. Brandishing a gun at a couple of old ladies out for a walk in Sacramento... what a manly thing to do. That's why you and Jake got along so well. You're both cut from the same cloth. Your heart is as ugly as his."

Sophia ran out the front door just as José body slammed Tony to the floor.

"Let's go," Derek said, grabbing my arm and pulling me around the melee. Some of the family stayed inside to try to break it up, while others filed out with us. I searched for Sophia. The dusty cloud down the driveway indicated she'd driven away in a hurry.

Derek pulled out his phone and dialed 911 as the fight spilled outside. Fists flew, blood spattered, and the air filled with ripe cursing and yells. I turned away and buried my head in Derek's chest while he put his arm around me.

The funeral for the man who had been so awful in life had turned uglier than I could have ever imagined. Even from the grave, Jake Martinez left a path of destruction.

Two hours later, the police had taken everyone's statement. I'd listened as Tony laid out how he'd killed his brother. He'd had lunch earlier in the day with Jake at his home and sprinkled some cyanide he'd made himself on Jake's turkey sandwich. It hadn't been enough though, which had led to Jake feeling as if he had the flu.

Jake had mentioned he had some paperwork to

do after closing, and Tony had known he always had nachos covered in his own homemade seasoning when at the restaurant. He'd ground his own herbs and peppers to make the unique concoction he'd kept in a special bottle.

No store-bought seasoning for Jake.

After his meal with Jake, Tony had visited Martinez's Mexican Fiesta and added the ground up apple seeds to the spice bottle only Jake used just to make certain his brother would ingest enough to die. Tony knew Jake would add his herb blend to the nachos—he always piled it on—and he'd given himself plenty to finish off the job.

Tony confessed that if it had been discovered as a murder, he'd hoped José went down for it. The fact the police had screwed up so badly and arrested Carla mortified him.

José and Tony were cuffed and driven off to the sheriff's department. Byron had been one of the officers who responded to the call, and he said nothing to me, but tossed plenty of angry glares my way as I stood hand in hand with Derek.

At some point, he'd have to get over me and move on with his life.

"Let's swing by the restaurant," I said to Derek as we left. "I want to see if Sophia is there."

We found her car parked out back. "I'm going in," I said. "Would you mind waiting here just for a bit?"

Derek squeezed my palm and shook his head. "Only for you."

I leaned over and gave him a quick kiss. "Thanks."

After lightly tapping on the door, I waited and hoped Sophia would answer. I knocked again, and after the third time, she finally did.

"What are you doing here?" she said with a harsh glare. "I want to be left alone!"

She may be angry at my intrusion, but she'd also been crying and probably needed a friend.

"I'm sure you do, but I wanted to talk to you for a minute. I have something to show you inside."

Her anger turned to confusion, and she motioned me to enter.

We sat in the first booth by the kitchen and she wiped her face with a napkin.

"I know today was hard," I said. "But I hope it can be the catalyst for you to make some changes in your life."

She stared at me for a long moment. "I liked my life just fine beforehand when I didn't know my boyfriend held up old women and my uncle wasn't a killer."

"Isn't it better to know the truth? What if José lost his temper and actually laid his hands on you?"

"I don't know," she whispered. "I feel like the rug has been pulled out from under me."

"It has, Sophia. Can I tell you a quick story?"

She nodded.

"My father wasn't a bad guy, but he wasn't a very nice person. He never had time for me. He died unexpectedly and I thought my world had ended. My mom promised me that things would only get better for us. We moved to Louisiana, and they did. They got a lot better. Maybe you just need to leave everything behind and start over."

"With what?" Sophia asked, throwing up her hands. "I'm the owner of this restaurant! We're finally starting to make money, but I don't have anything saved. I barely have two cents to rub together."

"What about all your new appliances?"

"Credit," she mumbled. "All of it was bought on my dad's credit."

"Come here," I said, standing. "Follow me."

It sounded like Sophia wasn't aware of the stack of cash hidden in the booth where her father died. If she was, I didn't know how I would explain my knowledge of it.

I led her over to the table where her father had been killed and yanked up the seat, then tossed it to the floor. Sophia gasped when I leaned over and began pulling out stacks of money and setting them on the table.

"How did you know about this?" she shrieked. I could hear it in her voice—she had no idea about the treasure.

"It doesn't matter," I replied. "But it's yours. It's your ticket out of here. It's a way for you to start a new life."

Behind me I could hear Sophia crying again. I continued to scoop out the bricks of money and set them on the table. When I got to the bottom, I found a few pictures.

One was of Carla kissing a man I didn't recognize... a man who wasn't her husband, Mac. I pulled it out and stuffed it in the front of my pants, hoping Sophia didn't see me doing so.

I stood upright and turned to the young woman. "You've been surrounded by bad men your entire life. You loved your father, but he hurt a lot of people and wasn't a good role model for you. José is trash. Your uncle... he's a killer. Run, Sophia." I pointed at the table. "Take all this money and run. Start a new life. Travel. Go play in the ocean. See the pyramids.

Your life doesn't have to be a string of horrible events any longer. Find out who you are, who you want to be. The restaurant will be here if you ever want to come back."

She stared at me wide-eyed, and my sympathies for her rose. Sophia had had it rough—her mother dying, her father instigating horrible acts against others, being in love with a criminal, her father's murder. She deserved a break.

The tears started again and she threw her arms around me. "Thank you," she whispered. "Thank you for everything."

"Leave soon," I replied, patting her back. "Don't let anyone convince you to stay. Do this for yourself."

"I will."

22

THE NEXT TWO weeks passed in a blur. Sophia did leave town and Martinez's Mexican Restaurant was left locked up. Maybe one day she'd return, or maybe not. I just hoped she straightened out her life.

Sheriff Connor released Carla without an apology and defended his actions by saying he simply went where the evidence took him. It was very difficult for me to write the article without insinuating that he was an incompetent boob who cared nothing about the case, only his reelection.

When Carla no longer had a job, Debbie convinced her to join her at the bakery since the second person she'd hired had quit. Carla finally acquiesced, and things seemed to be going well. Debbie stuck to the baking while Carla took over the business side. Debbie was thrilled with the arrangement, especially when Carla announced she'd found ways to help her save about a thousand dollars every month without cutting the quality of her products.

The picture I'd found of Carla and the mystery man burned in my purse. I wanted to confront her and find out the story behind it, but I also realized it wasn't any of my business. I didn't even discuss it with Derek.

But the afternoon of the Halloween dance, I stopped at the bakery for a coffee and realized Carla and I were alone. I pulled out the picture and set it down on the table between us. She gasped and stared at it for a moment, then crinkled it up in her palm. She wouldn't meet my gaze.

"That was at the very bottom of the booth with the money at Martinez's Mexican Restaurant," I said quietly. Carla never would have seen it unless she emptied all the money like I had. "Why did Jake have that picture?

Carla sighed and shook her head. "It was taken when I first started working at the restaurant. Mac was out of town and... and we weren't getting along. We were actually talking about divorcing. That guy... I don't even remember his name. He was a server at the restaurant. We flirted. He made me feel everything Mac didn't at that time. Then, one day, he kissed me."

Her story caused me to squirm in my chair because I had an idea of where it was going and I wasn't sure I wanted to hear the rest.

"I don't need to know the details, Carla. I just wanted you to have this."

"No, I want to tell someone because it's weighed so heavily on my heart."

"Are you sure?"

Carla nodded. "That was taken one night after closing. Jake saw him kiss me, then told him to do it again. We were all laughing. It was a silly thing, but that kiss touched a place in me that Mac hadn't reached in a long time."

"So you kissed him again?"

"Yes. That's when Jake snapped the picture."

"Then what happened? Why did Jake keep it?"

Tears welled in her eyes as she shook her head. "About a year later, I'd asked for a raise. Mac and I had worked through our problems. Jake told me I wouldn't get what I asked for, and he added that if I ever tried to leave the restaurant, he'd show the picture to Mac."

As her tears slid down her cheeks, I closed my

eyes. The depths of Jake Martinez's depravity never failed to surprise me.

Mac worshipped the ground Carla walked on, and he would be devastated to see the picture.

"I tried everything to either get him to give me a raise or let me go. I got his costs down and his profits up. I wanted out of there so badly, but he threatened me time and time again, reminding me he would make sure Mac saw the picture if I tried to leave."

"He extorted you," I whispered as I clenched my fists.

"He did. Please don't tell Mac."

"I won't, Carla. That picture isn't any of my business. You keep it, and I promise you, my lips are sealed."

Our gazes locked for a moment and Carla smiled. "Thank you. I appreciate that. I always wondered where he kept the picture and if it would turn up again. I'm so glad you're the one who found it."

"Me, too. And I promise I won't say a word about it to anyone. Your relationship with Mac is your business."

Carla nodded. "We were going through a really bad time, but things are good now. I can't imagine my life without him. The whole thing was just stupid, and if he ever saw the picture, it would destroy him. I never want to hurt him like that, and that's why I stayed at the restaurant."

"I understand. No one is perfect. We all do dumb things."

"You're right," she said with a sigh. "I really feel like a weight has been lifted from my shoulders now that I have this." She glanced down at her fist. "I think I need to burn it."

She stood and went in back, then returned with a bowl and some matches. As the picture burned, I couldn't help but wonder if the smoke and fumes contained cyanide.

"How are things going here?" I asked, glancing around. "You haven't killed each other, so I assume Debbie isn't driving you completely crazy."

"Debbie isn't as bad as a boss as I thought she'd be," Carla said with a laugh. "At least she's nothing like Jake."

"Yeah, you hit the worst of the worst with him as a boss." I grinned and reached across the table to squeeze her hand. "I'm glad to hear everything is going well, and I'm so happy you're out of that horrible situation."

"So am I. Frankly, I'm glad Sophia left town and it's shuttered. It was a toxic place to be."

We sipped our coffee in silence for a moment as the flames completely died down and ashes were all that was left.

"Are you and Mac going to the dance tonight?" I asked.

"We are. Will we see you there?"

"Yes. Derek and I will be attending together."

"We're going to have so much fun!" Carla said with a squeal.

I had to admit, I was pretty excited about the Halloween dance as well.

THE COMMUNITY CENTER had been decorated in black and orange with strobe lights that cast shadows in every dark corner. Balloons floated at the ceiling while streamers hung at the entrance and around the walls. The town had pulled together a potluck, and the tables lined with food all set my stomach growling. Up on the stage, a DJ played music.

Derek and I had decided to go as Gomez and Morticia Addams, the parents from the Addams Family. I have to admit, we looked really good. Derek had greased back his black hair and wore a fake mustache. I found a long black wig and dress. Even though I wasn't as thin as Morticia, I still felt darn sexy.

We arrived to find Mac, Carla, and Debbie saving us seats at a table. Carla and Mac were dressed as salt and pepper shakers, while Debbie wore a chef's hat and apron. Derek brought over two cups of juice, and I quickly drank mine, then snuck in some of Mac's hard cider. I rarely consumed alcohol, so it went directly to my head, giving me the giggles.

Derek and I danced a bit, but not too much because my costume and wig made me hot and sweaty.

About halfway through, the lights came up, the music stopped, and I turned to find the mayor at the microphone dressed as the Hulk ready to give a speech.

"Welcome, Tri-Towns!" he began. "It's so great to have everyone here!"

People applauded and hooted, and I had a feeling there was more than one flask of an adult beverage going around.

"This year, we've decided to do something different. I've appointed a secret judging committee whose members have been walking around looking at all your costumes, and we've come up with three finalists. The rest of you will decide the winner!"

Thunderous applause and squeals of delight filled the air.

"Our first finalists for the couple's competition are... Derek York and Tilly Bordeaux!"

I gasped as hoots and hollers filled the air. Derek grabbed my hand and we walked to the stage as the other two finalists were announced. My palms became sweaty and my body trembled when Burt Reynolds and Pamela Anderson walked up to the stage, followed by Han Solo and Princess Leia.

"We've got our three couples up here," the mayor continued, "and I must say, you all look fantastic. If it were up to me, I wouldn't be able to judge, so that's why I'm going to ask the audience. By a show of applause, which couple has your favorite costume? Is it Burt Reynolds and Pamela Anderson?"

Screams and yells echoed around the space as I stared out at the sea of faces. Some I recognized, others I didn't either because I didn't know them, or I couldn't place them through their masks and makeup.

I really wanted to win. A silly costume contest? Yes. But as I stood up on that stage with my boyfriend, a fierce sense of competitiveness took over my being.

When the applause died down, the mayor asked, "What about Han Solo and Princess Leia?"

My heart sank when the cheers became so loud, it was almost deafening. We'd never beat that.

"And finally, we have Gomez and Morticia Addams!" the mayor yelled.

I almost covered my ears, the noise becoming so thunderous as I began jumping up and down. We'd won!

Derek swept me up into his arms and spun me around while both of us laughed. When he set me down, I looked out into the audience to see Carla and Debbie standing on the table waving and screaming. Mac sat beneath them smiling, but shaking his head, as if he couldn't believe the shenanigans going on above him.

"Congratulations, Tilly and Derek!" the mayor said when the room quieted down. "You guys look amazing! Unfortunately, we don't have a prize for you except the bragging rights."

The audience laughed, but the prize was enough for me.

"I was wondering if I could say something," Derek said.

The mayor handed him the microphone and nodded but seemed just as puzzled as me. "Go right ahead."

"Thanks," Derek said, and then he cleared his throat. Beads of sweat formed on his brow as he turned to me. "Tilly, from the moment I saw you standing in my front yard holding a baseball bat over your shoulder while threatening to beat me with it, I've been attracted to you."

When he dropped to one knee, I gasped and took a step back. "What are you doing?" I hissed.

"You're the first person I think about when I wake up every day. I can't wait to see your smile, to hear your laughter, to hold you in my arms. You bring out a joy in me that I never imagined could be possible."

I glanced out at Carla and Debbie, who still stood on the table. They both held their hands up to their mouths in surprise.

At least they weren't in on it.

"We've only been dating for a short period of time, but I've also learned that life goes by really fast and it's important to live each day to its fullest. I'm in love with you and want to spend the rest of my days with you. I've never been so sure of anything in my life."

The crowd cheered while tears welled in my

eyes. Derek pulled a little black box out of his pocket. When he opened it, a gold ring with a small diamond gleamed under the stage lights.

I knew what was coming, and I suddenly felt very sick. Darkness encroached on my peripheral vision, the room began to spin, and my knees weakened. My stomach rolled, and I realized all that cider I had drunk was about to make a reappearance in front of the Tri-Town people and all over the man professing his love to me.

"Tilly Bordeaux, I know I'm being impulsive, but I also know you are who I want. Will you please marry me?"

ABOUT THE AUTHOR

Carly Winter is the pen name for a USA Today best-selling and award-winning romance author. When not writing, she enjoys spending time with her family, reading and enjoying the fantastic Arizona weather (except summer - she doesn't like summer). She does like dogs, wine and chocolate and wishes Christmas happened twice a year. To be notified of new releases, book recommendations, to learn more about Carly and for your chance to win a gift card every month, please visit CarlyWinterCozyMysteries.com